Plus One at an Amish Wedding

Heartfelt Romance

Runaway Romance
Follow Your Heart
Plus One at an Amish Wedding

Plus One at an Amish Wedding

BY MIRALEE FERRELL

Plus One at an Amish Wedding
Published by Mountain Brook Ink
White Salmon, WA U.S.A.

All rights reserved. Except for brief excerpts for review purposes, no part of this book may be reproduced or used in any form without written permission from the publisher.

The website addresses shown in this book are not intended in any way to be or imply an endorsement on the part of Mountain Brook Ink, nor do we vouch for their content.

This story is a work of fiction. All characters and events are the product of the author's imagination.

ISBN 978-1-953957-33-7
© 2022 Miralee Ferrell

The Team: Miralee Ferrell, Tim Pietz, Kristen Johnson, Cindy Jackson

Cover Design: Alyssa Roat & American Cinema International

Mountain Brook Ink is an inspirational publisher offering fiction you can believe in.

Printed in the United States of America

Dedication

To my entire family who have always believed in me and support me every step of my journey. I love you with all of my heart

And to my readers . . . without your continued support of my writing, there would be no more stories. Thank you!

Acknowledgments

Wouldn't it be wonderful if books wrote themselves and we could sit back and have a new one from our favorite author come out as soon as we finished reading the last one? Trust me, that would be amazing for the author as well. There are times writers sit and stare at the computer screen, wondering what will come next, wondering if the words will ever come to fill that blank page in our Word document. Sometimes it's a matter of minutes, other times, a matter of days or more, which can turn into agony for said writer. I know. I've been stuck in that wilderness of no words in the past, and it's not fun.

Thankfully, this book didn't hit those snags, and it was mostly due to the brilliant work of the script writer, D.F.W. Buckingham. Some of my books that became movies were collaborative efforts where I was actively involved in the storyline, others were my book from the start, but this one truly belongs to the scriptwriter. I was asked to write the book for this movie by Chevonne O'Shaughnessy, my producer and co-owner of American Cinema Inspires, and my friend since 2014 when we first started working together on book/movie projects. This book wraps up a three-book set of Amish books, and it was a joy to write. Of course, much of the book is mine—the script is only 15,000 words, and this book is 45,000 words, so a lot has been added and fleshed out, including a closer look into one of the character's hearts that isn't shown in the movie.

But the heart of the book came from the scriptwriter, and I'm extremely grateful for the talent that shines through.

I didn't have the chance to visit the set while the movie was being shot. This is one I truly wanted to attend, since Galadriel Steinman, the actress who plays April has appeared in three of my movies so far, and I have yet to meet her. She's become my favorite actor from all of my movies (5 so far) and if you watch the movie, I think you'll agree she's perfect for the part.

My editor, Fay Lamb, jumped in fast at the last minute and zipped through my edit on short notice. I experienced a number of setbacks while writing this book, and as I'm typing this, I'm only three weeks from when it's supposed to release—that's cutting it way too fine. I so appreciate editors who are able to do a fast, clean job, as well as the entire team at Mountain Brook Ink, my publishing house, and Alyssa Roat, who used the art provided by American Cinema and created a lovely cover.

Thank you all from the bottom of my heart. This book-to-movie and movie-to-book journey has been amazing from start to finish. I don't know what the future holds with my writing—at this point, I plan to go back to finish my final kids' horse novel and then write another historical romance set in the Old West (my true love in writing), but who knows? Maybe there's another movie in my future someday. If not, I'm very content. I've had far more than most authors have had, and I'm so very grateful to the Lord for bringing it all to pass.

Chapter One

APRIL MONROE STOOD IN FRONT OF her apartment gazing first left and then right—should she walk the few blocks to her favorite coffee shop in downtown New York City or head straight to work at Lenox Hospital? Her boss, Dr. Schneider, was a stickler for being punctual, but if she hurried, she'd still arrive at work with at least ten minutes to spare. With the stress levels Dr. S. provided at work, an Americano espresso was exactly what the doctor ordered—or rather, he probably would frown on it deeply, but since she was a doctor as well, she would order it and enjoy every last drop.

On her days off, she enjoyed strolling past Central Park or even cutting across the expansive lawns and stopping to watch the ducks and geese on the ponds. That was the one part of New York she truly loved—the park, with the horse-drawn carriages meandering past, the vendors with the mouth-watering fragrances of food wafting on the air, and the sight of children running and playing as though they didn't have a care in the world. Of course, many of them probably didn't, but there was a dark side to any city, and unfortunately, she'd seen kids come into the hospital that didn't have a happy childhood.

She picked up her pace. No time today to cut through the park. If she wanted that Americano, she'd have to walk double-time and hope the line wasn't too long. She pushed through the glass door and strode to the counter. There was already a queue of people who appeared to have ordered and one man down at the other registering placing his order now. Since hers was simple, hopefully they'd get to it fast.

Ten minutes later, she looked at her watch for at least the third time. This was normally her favorite coffee spot, but not when they were running late with her order. She bit her lip. Dr. Schneider would throw a fit if she walked in even five minutes after the hour. Better to forgo her breakfast-of-sorts and be on time.

She started to head for the door when welcome words carried over the counter. "Order up!" The barista held a cup in the air and then set it down on the top of the glass case separating her area from the customers teeming inside the close quarters between a round table and the cash register. "Double cappuccino, almond milk."

April's shoulders sagged. She'd been sure that one would be hers. She took a step closer. "Sorry to bother you when you're busy, but will mine be much longer? If not, I'll need to cancel as I can't be late for work."

The barista wiped the back of her hand across her cheek, brushing at a wisp of hair that had fallen out of her ponytail. "Yeah, it shouldn't be much longer."

The guy April had seen ordering at the same time she had smiled and cocked his head to the side. "The espresso machine has been giving them fits, and they can't get a repairman in to fix it until later today." He grinned, and the smile lit up his face.

Wow. When she'd first seen him, she thought him nice looking, but that grin made her heart do a flip. "Thanks. How do you know so much? Do you work here?" Dark hair, slender build, not too tall, but taller than she was, very cute smile . . . *hey, hold it*. What was she thinking? She didn't have time for romance or any distractions in her life. She'd finished her residency two years ago and didn't feel like she'd really found her footing yet at Lenox. Most days, she put in long hours, which extended even longer with having to keep patient records updated. Nope. Romance definitely didn't fit into her schedule. She shot another peek at the man. Early thirties, maybe a couple of years her senior, and nicely dressed, but nothing fancy. Not that it mattered.

Now he laughed outright. "Nope. Just frequent the place a lot, and I happened to be around when the machine went on the fritz and they called the repairman. Nobody here was happy when he said he couldn't come until tomorrow. They've been limping along as best they can, but it has slowed things a bit."

"I appreciate that, thanks." Did he have a slight accent? She wasn't sure, but his voice was soft, pleasant, and definitely courteous to a fault. In fact, it was one of the rare times in this city that she felt truly comfortable talking with a guy close to her own age. Most people ignored you, or the guys tried to hit on you, but this one was different. A good kind of different that she could get used to.

"Order up!" The barista set another cup on the glass countertop. "Americano, extra cream."

April swung around and then let her breath

out in a whoosh. *Finally.* She reached for the cup only to rub her hand against the guy with the great smile who reached it first.

He raised one brow. "Sorry, this one's mine."

"Uh, no. That's what I ordered." She reached for it again, but his penetrating gaze stopped her.

"So did I." He pulled his hand back. "There's only one way to solve this. I also ordered a cinnamon..."

"Cinnamon raisin bagel to go." The barista placed a small white sack next to the drink.

April reached for the sack. "That is definitely mine. I ordered an Americano, extra cream, and a cinnamon raisin bagel to go."

"Same here. So, now what do we do?" At least the man had the decency to not reach for the cup or the sack again.

A couple of customers behind them chuckled, and April couldn't help but smile at the irony. She was going to be late, and someone else ordered exactly what she had. What were the odds? "Go ahead. I saw you ordering when I started placing my order, so it's probably yours."

He shook his head. "No. Ladies first."

She wanted to grab it and dash out the door, but that would be beyond rude. "You're sure?"

"Absolutely. You mentioned you're going to be late for work, and I'm not, so it only makes sense." He reached forward and plucked the bag and coffee off the counter and pressed it into her hands.

When April took it, her fingers brushed his and she almost yelped. *Yikes.* She knew there was no such thing as love at first sight, but this guy was too good to be true—and there was definitely attraction at first sight. "Thank you so much. I really appreciate it." She took the container and her bagel and walked to the door, pushing it open with her shoulder while glancing back. Yep, he was looking at her as well. A shame she didn't have time to find out his name or learn more about him, but work called. She sighed. Hopefully, she'd make it to the hospital in time.

The next day, Jesse Hardin pushed through the doors of the operating room at the veterinarian clinic where he worked. Then he slipped the surgical mask up on his face and straightened his surgical gown. He needed to get the young woman from the coffee shop out of his mind and get his focus on the little sheltie that needed its broken leg repaired. Thankfully, it wasn't a bad enough break that it had done permanent nerve or tendon damage, and the young dog would make a full recovery. That was the satisfying part of his job. He almost shuddered remembering the dog they couldn't save last week. It had run across the road and had been hit by a car.

A vet assistant stood beside a small table with the sheltie laying on top. He'd already been put under and appeared to be peacefully sleeping. "Dr. Jesse?"

He looked up and smiled, happy that he'd finally convinced the staff at the clinic to stop calling him Dr. Hardin. "Everything ready for me?"

"Yes, sir." Thankfully, she was one of the older, married assistants and not the new, young one who blushed every time he spoke to her. He almost chuckled at the memory of the young woman yesterday debating with him whose coffee it was—she certainly hadn't blushed when he spoke to her. In fact, he'd almost have said sparks were shooting from her lovely hazel eyes. Actually, they may have been a rich brown—he couldn't be sure. They seemed to change with her mood.

"Doctor?" His assistant gave him a quizzical stare. "Are you ready to start?"

He moved to the side of the table and nodded. "Sorry, yes. Let's get to work and see if we can leave this little guy without a limp."

Two hours later, he stripped off his gown and mask and headed for the breakroom for a much-needed coffee. Not quite the Americano he'd ordered yesterday, but it would do. Somehow, he'd enjoyed the espresso even more knowing he was drinking the same thing the cute woman had ordered and was probably drinking it at the same time as he. He propped his feet up on a nearby chair and closed his eyes for a moment, trying to get his muscles to relax after two hours of constant vigilance in the O.R. He loved his work, but when it was over, he was more than ready to relax for a few minutes. Too bad he hadn't thought to ask that young woman for her phone number, but it still made him uncomfortable to do that kind of thing. Maybe one day he'd get past his strict upbringing, but yesterday hadn't been the day. He'd opened his mouth to say something when she'd gotten to the door and glanced back, but all he could manage was a weak smile. What an idiot he was. In a town this size, the chance of seeing her again was slim—although he could probably go to the same coffee shop, and he might get lucky. He smiled. Having a plan was a good thing—or as his *maam* would say, a *goot* thing, indeed.

have worn my best running

Chapter Two

APRIL SAT NEXT TO THE OLDER woman in her late fifties in the clinic side of Lenox Hospital. She loved practicing general family medicine at the clinic associated with and housed in the hospital, even if Dr. Schneider oversaw the personnel in both places. If only he wasn't such an old pill and a stickler for moving patients in and out quickly. She believed in the personal touch. Her mother had always told her how much it had meant to her when she had breast cancer that her doctor had taken the time to explain everything to her and assuage her fears, even though the cancer came back years later and took her mom's life. It was her mother's influence that had convinced her to go into medicine in the first place. She'd seriously considered nursing, but she wanted to do everything she could to make the same kind of difference in others' lives in the same way the doctor had who'd been such a comfort to her mother.

Mrs. Beauregard sat fingering her pearl necklace, her brows scrunched together as though worried or deep in thought while April listened to the older woman's heart for several seconds.

April let the stethoscope fall back to its place on her chest and then helped Mrs. Beauregard off the table and over to her chair. Thankfully, she appeared steady on her feet and not shaky or weak.

April settled into her chair a few feet from her patient and leaned forward. "The feeling in your chest . . . is it more of a sharp pain, a heaviness, a dull ache, or . . .? Can you describe it for me and tell me how long it's been going on?"

"More of a tightness, I think." She pursed her lips and then continued. "It only lasts a few minutes, but it usually happens after I take Coco on her walk. That's my little dog. She's a Pomeranian, and she's still pretty young. It's been a challenge to completely housebreak her, you know, so she has to go out more frequently than I'm used to. She also walks a bit faster than I normally do, so I sometimes get a little out of breath."

April looked at her laptop and reviewed the

notes from Mrs. Beauregard's last couple of visits. "Your cholesterol has crept up over your last few checkups, and your blood pressure is higher than I like to see it. I'd like to schedule an ECG and possibly a stress test. That might be more than is needed, but I'd prefer to be safe if you're all right with that?"

"Oh, dear." Mrs. Beauregard placed a hand over her heart. "You don't think I'm dying, do you? I don't know who'd take care of my darling Coco if something happened to me."

April did her best to keep a smile from tipping up her lips. This dear woman was a worrier, and she'd have to do her best to reassure her. She met the concern in her patient's eyes with a compassionate gaze. "I think it's a very mild case, and I believe we can keep it that way. You are nowhere near dying, and I don't want you to worry. I'm going to give you a few things that you should change in your diet, and I want you to take more walks . . . not just when Coco needs to go out, but maybe a little more often and a bit longer. Get to the point where you're not winded, and you'll find a few pounds dropping off and your blood pressure and cholesterol lowering, as well as any potential heart risks, will more than likely start disappearing as well." She snapped her laptop shut and stood. "I want you and Mr. Beauregard to have a lot more happy years together, assuming you want to, that is?"

Mrs. Beauregard chuckled and nodded. "Indeed, I do. And I appreciate the wake-up call, too."

"Good." April headed toward the door. "Plus, I want you to outlive Coco, so you won't have to worry about her care. Come on. I'll walk you out and make sure you get those tests scheduled. I sent the information up to the front but just in case they have any questions."

She walked with the older woman, keeping pace with her shorter stride. They rounded a corner and almost bumped into Dr. Schneider.

He came to an abrupt stop and scowled, not a pleasant look on his thin face. "Dr. Monroe." His shoe started tapping on the floor as he peered over the top of his wire-rimmed glasses. "Why aren't you in Room 223?"

April blinked a couple of times, trying to clear her mind and remember what his question might be referring to. "I'm sorry. Umm . . . what's in Room 223?"

He narrowed his eyes, and his fingers began echoing the tapping, only they hit the file he was holding, with an annoying rhythm. "Mr. Shepherd. Waiting. Patiently. But I'm guessing his patience is going to wear thin soon. You need to get in there. You're running late. Again."

"Oh. I'm sorry. I thought his appointment wasn't until four thirty." She looked at her watch. "That's another fifteen minutes."

"It was moved up. I'm trying to help you keep shorter appointments. I'm afraid you're spending too much time with the patients." He looked pointedly at Mrs. Beauregard. "You are finished, are you not?"

April did her best to keep her tone civil. She could deal with his irritating, rude behavior when it was aimed at her, but every hackle rose when it was aimed at one of her patients. "I'll just be a second, Doctor. I'm helping Mrs. Beauregard schedule her ECG."

"No need. That's what reception is for. Please get to room 223 immediately." He didn't so much as smile or tip his head before he stalked off down the hall.

Mrs. Beauregard's mouth gaped open for a couple of seconds before she snapped it shut and turned to April. "A real charmer, isn't he? I'll bet he has a great bed-side manner with the patients."

"Sorry, Mrs. B. Dr. Schneider was only being himself. Thankfully, he's only in charge of the hospital staff, and patients don't have to interact with him." She grimaced. "Except for you, that is." She sighed. "Maybe one of these days, he'll find out life is more than just keeping everyone efficient."

April and Mrs. B. hurried to the front desk where April turned her over to their very competent receptionist. "Molly will help you, and if you have any questions or concerns, you're welcome to call me."

"Thank you, dear, but I'm sure that won't be necessary. I'll take all your advice to heart."

April spun around ready to dash to room 223.

"Aunt April, Aunt April, wait!" A boy cried behind her, and she whipped around again. Her nephew, Zack, ran across the lobby carrying his little black and brown beagle. "Scout and I were playing ball at the park, and he ran out in the road after the ball. It was my fault. I threw it way too hard. Mom isn't home, and I didn't know what to do. I was at the park across the road from the hospital, and, and . . ."

"Take a deep breath, buddy. Did Scout get hurt?" April stepped close and inspected the dog who wasn't moving.

"Yes. A car hit him. The man tried to stop, but his tire clipped him. The man rolled down his window and yelled that I needed to keep my dog on a leash. Then he left. He didn't even try to help me. Can you help him? You're a doctor!"

April ran her hand across the top of Scout's head, concerned when the little dog only whimpered. "Honey, I'm not that kind of doctor. We need to find a vet, but I don't have animals, and I'm not sure where to take him." She turned toward the receptionist. "Molly, can you do a search and see where the closest veterinarian clinic is?"

"Sure, Dr. Monroe." Molly turned to her computer.

"Take him to my vet. It's very close, and he's excellent. I won't trust anyone with my Coco but him. He's three blocks from here, on Eighty-Second. Tell him I sent you. I'm sure they'll get you right in." Mrs. Beauregard reached out and touched Scout's head.

"Thank you so much, Mrs. B. I owe you." April slipped her arm around Zack's shoulders and headed toward the door. "Oops. Molly, could you please send someone to room 223 and let Mr. Shepherd know I've had a family emergency? I'll get back as soon as I can, but if he wants to reschedule, it's fine. Please tell him I'm so sorry."

Molly waved her toward the door. "Will do. Now scram, and get that poor little guy to the vet. Call me as soon as you can and let me know if you're coming back and how Scout is doing." Her warm brown eyes were filled with warmth and concern.

"Thanks." April breathed a prayer on the way out the door. "Please Lord, keep Scout safe, and give us the right vet who can take care of whatever is wrong with him. It will break Zack's heart if he loses this little guy."

Jesse had barely finished his coffee and was stretching his back when another vet tech rushed into the room. "Sorry to bother you, Dr. Jesse, but I'm not sure what to do. We've seen the last patient for the day, and we were almost ready to close, but a woman and little boy brought in their dog. The boy said it was hit by a car, and I can tell he's very upset. Do you want to take a look at him?" She bit her lip. "I know you're tired after that long surgery, but the vet tech already went home, and there's only an assistant here. I'm so sorry."

"Nothing to be sorry about at all. Show them into a room, and I'll wash up and be right there. It's too far to the next clinic, and they might be closed by the time they arrived. I don't mind being home a little later than usual." He gave a wry smile as she rushed off. It wasn't like he had anyone to hurry home to, after all.

A couple of minutes later, he headed to the exam room, opened the door, and stepped inside. A woman and small boy were bent over the beagle curled in the boy's lap. The woman raised her head, and a jolt seemed to pass through her as her mouth formed a small O. "You. What...why?"

"Hello, I'm Jesse Hardin, a veterinarian at this clinic. Let's take a look at this little guy, shall we?" He turned his attention to the boy and his dog. "Can you let my assistant take your pup and put him on the table so I can see how he's doing? I promise she'll be very gentle."

The little boy nodded and watched closely

while Jesse's assistant carefully lifted the pup onto the table. "What's his name?" Jesse glanced at the boy and then at his mom. "Can you tell me how he got hurt?"

"My name is Zack, and he's Scout." He pointed at the beagle. "I was playing fetch in the park, and I threw the ball. It rolled out into the street, and before I could run and catch Scout, he went after it. A car hit him, and he fell down and started crying."

The young woman from the coffee shop took a step closer. "Zack ran across the street to the hospital where I work and found me as I was walking out a patient. I brought them straight here."

Jesse smiled as he prodded gently at the dog's hip. "We're going to take a couple of X-rays, but I think he might have a broken back leg. I'll give him a pain killer first to make it easier on him, but we'll probably have to put a cast on it. Do you think Scout has a favorite color, Zack?"

The boy didn't even hesitate. "Dogs are colorblind, but I like red."

"Red it is, then. You and your mom can wait here until we're done with the X-rays and the cast. Then I'll bring Scout back to you."

"She's not my mom." Zack giggled. "She's my aunt, and she's not married. My mom was at work, and Aunt April was closer, so I went to the hospital where she works. She's a doctor too, but she said she can't work on animals, or she would have fixed him."

Jesse's brows went up, and he shot a glance at April. *Single. Nice. And a doctor. Go figure.* "Scout will need to go home with pain pills. I'll give you the instructions. If you can pass those along to Zack's parents, that would be great."

She heaved a sigh. "I'm so relieved he'll be all right. Yes, I'll take both of them home when you finish and give everything to my sister. Thank you so much for seeing us, Doctor."

He grinned as the assistant left the room with Scout. "It's Jesse. I feel like we're already old friends after a coffee emergency and now this." He walked toward the door and swung it open and then turned back. "In fact, when you get off work, maybe you'd like to have coffee with me? At the same spot where we ran into each other?" He couldn't believe it. What was the chance he'd run into April again, and here in his clinic, of all places? *Thank You, Lord.* He hadn't really been on close speaking teams to the Almighty in the last few years, but somehow, it seemed the right time to at least say thanks.

Soft color rose in her cheeks. "I'd like that. Very much."

Chapter Three

Six Months Later

APRIL SAT ACROSS THE TABLE IN the candlelit restaurant, thinking back over the last few months since she'd started dating Jesse. It started out slow, but in the last few weeks, it had taken a bit of a more serious turn, and she felt her heartrate increase as she looked into his warm brown eyes. He reached across the table, took her hand, and gave it a soft squeeze. Was he going to propose? Was she ready for such a big step? There were so many things they hadn't talked about . . . like his family, his past, where he'd grown up. It seemed as if they mostly talked about her, and she still had so many questions.

He gave her fingers one more tender squeeze, released her, and leaned back in his chair. "That was a fantastic dinner. It's still boggles me that I met you, as I figured I'd never see you again. I wanted to run out of the coffee shop after you, only to have you and Zack come into the clinic with Scout."

Well, that wasn't what she'd expected, but maybe he was leading up to more? "I know what you mean. I was just thinking the same thing. Scout doesn't even have a limp anymore, and my sister is so grateful." She gave a little smirk. "She's actually even more grateful you asked me out for coffee that evening. She'd about given up on me ever finding time to date someone, much less getting past the first date or two." April bit her lip. She'd almost said, "getting serious," but if he wasn't serious, she didn't want to send him bolting out the door.

He chuckled. "Yeah, I was getting pretty sick of my own company on my days off."

She leaned forward and met his eyes. "So . . . did you grow up around a lot of animals? Is that why you wanted to be a vet? You've never said much about your childhood or your family, and I've been wondering . . ."

He glanced away, not meeting her eyes. "Yeah. I've always had a heart for animals. We had a few when I was growing up." He reached into his pocket and pulled out an envelope. "I wanted to show you something." A smile lit his eyes this time, and he pulled out a small, velvet covered box.

She stifled a soft gasp wondering if she'd guessed correctly . . . but it was flat, not like a ring box at all. "What is this for? It's not my birthday."

"No—but it is six months today since our first date." He opened the box and held it so she could see it. "I've not seen you wear a lot of jewelry, but I thought this might be appropriate for the occasion."

A heart pendant hung on a delicate gold chain, and inside were tiny initials . . . A & J. He looked up when she didn't speak. "Too corny?" He started to pull it back across the table.

She reached out and stopped him. "Not a bit corny. My eyes were tearing up, and I was struggling to find the right words. I love it, Jesse. It's . . . perfect." And it was. She hadn't been ready for an engagement—the timing wasn't right, but this *was* perfect. She felt like a teen again with her first boyfriend who brought her a bouquet of daisies. Humbled. Touched. Romanced in all the right ways. A beautiful dinner in a romantic setting and a necklace that spoke volumes without asking for a lifetime commitment. What more could she ask?

April gave the new mother a warm smile as she rose from her chair in the examination room at Lenox Hospital. "Anemia's very common, especially with new moms. You can get more iron from meat, leafy vegetables, dry fruit . . . I also suggest a B12 vitamin. And of course, Susan, sleep as much as you can, when you can, to build up your strength." She opened the door and waited for the fatigued-looking young woman to step through.

Susan gave her a tired smile. "Thanks. I assumed I was wiped out all the time due to the baby. She's rolling over now and scooting, so she's more active and has to be watched more closely." She turned toward April as they stepped into the hallway. "Would you like to see a picture?" She dug around in her small purse, extracted a phone, and began to flip through it, barely waiting to hear an affirmative from April.

April peered over Susan's shoulder and smiled and then looked up at the sound of footsteps drawing near.

Dr. Schneider stopped a few feet away, a deep frown marring his thin face as he stared from Sally's phone to April and back. He cleared his throat, and Sally raised her head, but she didn't speak. More than likely, the sour expression he wore choked off any response she may have had.

"A word please, Dr. Monroe?" He looked pointedly at Sally.

"Um. Thank you for your advice today, Dr. April. I'd better get going."

"Give that baby girl a hug for me." April waved and smiled before turning her attention to Dr. Schneider. "What's up?"

He reached for the handle of the door she'd exited and swung it open, waited for her to enter, and then stepped in and shut it behind them. "I am sorry I'm having to say this yet again, but it appears you either aren't listening to me or don't care. Neither one is acceptable for a doctor on this staff. Our doctors do not have time to spend with individual patients."

"I did hear you, Doctor, and I do understand, but I believe I can better diagnose my patients when I know something about their background and their lives. Besides, they appreciate that I care, as well."

"Regardless, but we have quotas to fill and patients to treat. We do not befriend them or spend time on their personal lives. Is that clear?" He peered at her down his long, thin nose, his face scrunched in what was beginning to be a permeant scowl.

April steeled herself to do battle, but what was there to say? That he, as the head of their department, was wrong? That he didn't have the right to chastise her? That she'd continue to help her patients as she saw fit? None of those things would go over well with Dr. S. and could very well be the end of her job. Was that what she really wanted? She huffed out a soft breath instead. "Yes, Dr. Schneider. It's very clear."

A few days later, April jogged along a trail in Central Park while her older sister, May, panted behind her, struggling to keep up.

May's words drifted up the trail to April. "If you'd told me we were training for a timed marathon, I'd even to explore the non-Amish have worn my best running shoes and slugged down a bottle of energy drink before I left."

April slowed, not sure how she'd become so

absorbed in her own thoughts that she'd totally missed that May was dropping farther and farther behind. "Sorry, sis. I guess I wasn't paying attention." She slowed to a walk, allowing May to catch up.

"What's got you so riled?" May sucked in a deep breath. "Thanks. I could use a breather. My lungs were starting to hurt."

"Dr. Schneider. He's constantly nagging me about how much time I spend with my patients. *My* patients. What makes it worse is he often does it right in front of them, like he's trying to make them feel badly that they're taking too much of my time. It's embarrassing for both of us."

May stopped walking and put her hands on her knees. "Ugh. Now my back hurts too. Sorry, let me stretch for a minute." She reached for her toes for close to a minute and then slowly stood. "I guess first jobs stink sometimes, but I'm sorry that's happening to you."

April jogged in place as May continued to stretch. "He makes me feel like he wants me to be part of a huge, corporate machine rather than a doctor. The best way to treat a patient is to treat them like individual people. That takes time. It takes getting to know the person and what makes them tick. Maybe medicine isn't what I thought it was. Maybe I don't belong in this field."

May shook her head. "You do belong. You wanted to be a doctor from the time you were a kid. Remember all the stray animals you brought home, the bird you tried to fix when it broke its wing? Every time I got a cold or a sore throat, you immediately jumped into doctor mode. You always had a huge heart. That might be why you ended up with a veterinarian." She shot April a grin. "How are things with Mr. Wonderful, anyway?"

"He's great. I haven't had a chance to show you what he gave me for our six-month anniversary." She reached into her shirt and pulled out the engraved heart on the gold chain and showed it to May who touched it and oohed. "In fact, he's better than great. For the first time, I feel like I'm dating someone who really knows me—who hears my heart and is with me because of me—not because of my profession or anything physical." She bit her lip. "But . . ."

May started jogging in place beside April. "I'm ready to go, but let's take it a little slower the rest of the way. But what? You were saying?

There's something wrong with this perfect man?"

April giggled as they started down the path side by side. "I don't expect him to be perfect. It's just that . . . I don't feel like I really know him. He never talks about his past. I haven't met his family. In fact, he rarely mentions them. I know he has a younger brother and younger sister, but that's about it. We've been dating for six months, and I don't know a lot more than I did when I met him. That's not normal, is it?"

"Maybe there's a good reason he hasn't opened up yet. Not everyone grew up in a sheltered home, and he might have a painful past. Something he's not comfortable sharing yet."

"Yeah, that's what's making me nervous." Determined not to be silly, April pushed down the feeling of foreboding that had reared its snarling head. There definitely must be a good reason.

A couple of weeks after their anniversary dinner, Jesse sat across from April at what had become their favorite spot to meet when it wasn't a formal date—the coffee shop where they'd met. He'd been trying to take in what she was saying, but it hadn't totally registered. Somehow, he needed to tell her his news, but he'd better listen to her concerns first. He reached across and took her hand. "So things aren't working out at the hospital? Could it be time for a change?"

April curled her fingers into his as though his touch had reassured her. "But how would that look if I made a change this soon into my career? What do you think I should do, Jesse? I mean, not that I can't make my own decisions. I am an adult, after all." She squeezed his hand and then sat back, removing it from his grip. "I think I need to pray about it. I haven't been doing much of that lately. I'm so caught up in work all the time that I guess I've neglected that part of my life."

He grunted. "That makes two of us. Like, for years." He ran his hand over his face, still not sure how much to tell her.

April swirled her coffee with a swizzle stick. "You seem distracted and . . . worried? What's going on, Jesse?" Now it was her turn to reach across and grasp his hand. "I'm sorry for dumping all my hospital woes on you. Please tell me what's on your mind."

"Okay, here goes." He ran his thumb over the back of her knuckles. "I got a letter from my brother. He's getting married a week from now."

April's face brightened. "That's wonderful! I think you've mentioned your brother one time, but I don't know much about him . . . or your family. Younger brother, older? Wait . . . you mentioned younger in the past, but 'letter.' You meant, e-mail, right?" She tipped her head to the side and grinned.

"No." He shook his head. "I most definitely didn't say e-mail." He winced. "My family . . ." He paused and then sucked in a long, hard breath. "My family doesn't e-mail. They rarely use the telephone, unless it's an emergency, and they borrow a friend's or go to the store."

"Okay." April's brows rose.

"There's a lot you don't know about me. I'm sorry for keeping it quiet for so long, April. For not sharing more with you or explaining."

Her eyes grew wide and her grip on his hand tightened. "They aren't all in prison, are they?"

He almost hooted with laughter but chuckled instead. "I can see why you might jump to that conclusion since they're writing letters and not calling. No. I'm Amish, April. Born and raised."

"Come again?" April had brought her coffee mug to her mouth but set it down with a thump before taking a drink. "They're what? Does that mean you . . .?" The shock hit her hard. Maybe not as hard as if he'd come from a family of hardened criminals, but just the same . . . Amish? She had no idea what to even do with that information.

"I was raised Amish. I'm originally from Stone County, Pennsylvania. My family—my mom, dad, brother, sister—everyone I grew up with. Amish."

"That's unexpected. I mean, it's better than prison." She rolled her eyes. The last thing she wanted to do was discourage him from continuing since she'd been waiting for months to learn more about his family and his past. "Sorry. That is not what I meant. I'd love to hear more if you're all right sharing?"

"I entered *Rumspringa* when I was sixteen. That means I had two or three years to do what

I wanted to do, even to explore the non-Amish, *Englischer,* world until I decided whether I'd join the church and remain Amish or if I'd leave and go into the Englischer world. It took me nearly two years to decide. I loved my family so much, and I didn't want to leave. There were many things I loved about the Amish life, as well. The simplicity, the lack of pretensions, but there were things I wanted that they couldn't offer."

"Like going to college and becoming a vet?" She slid her hand back across the table and laid it in her lap but gave him a soft smile to let him know she wasn't trying to abandon him. This was all incredibly interesting. Jesse, Amish. Who would have guessed? What did she do with this information now that she knew? Would it change their relationship? She knew next to nothing about Amish ways—what they allowed with dating, or she supposed they called it courtship—but wait. He said he left, and he certainly didn't look Amish. She forced her attention back to him as he started speaking again.

"Exactly. Amish women become midwives, but no one is encouraged to become a doctor, a vet, or anything that involves leaving the Amish community and going away to college. That would entail a great risk that the person would take up modern ways and never return. We're encouraged to join the church, marry, raise children, and take up a trade within our community. That was never what I wanted. As you know, I have a deep love for animals as well as a desire to serve. I finally chose to leave and attend college and then veterinarian school."

Her mind spun, trying to take it all in. She'd always known there was something a bit different about Jesse. His quaint manners in a huge city where you rarely encountered his type of personality. His quiet demeanor. His . . . charm. There was no other way she could put it. Then another thought hit her, and she sat up in alarm. "Were you shunned? I saw a television documentary one time. I didn't watch it closely, but I remember something about Amish who leave being shunned."

"No. I made the decision to leave before joining the church, and shunning happens mostly with Old Order Amish. Amish are shunned if they join and then decide to leave or marry outside our faith—it can even happen if a married couple breaks their wedding vows and becomes unfaithful. Since I left when I was eighteen and hadn't taken any baptismal vows to the church, I can still go back to visit my family." A cloud seemed to cross his features. "I haven't been back over the last two years—only once since my dad's funeral." He glanced out the window. "I need to go home. It would mean so much to my brother for me to be there for his wedding, not to mention my mother and sister."

"I understand. I appreciate you sharing all of this with me."

He turned his attention back to her. "You're not freaked out?"

April smiled. "Not at all. Surprised, yes, freaked out, no. Not yet, anyway. Now if you totally change and start acting weird, I may need to rethink my reply." She thought he'd laugh and assure her that would never happen, but something like a look of pain flashed across his expression. "Jesse? Is there something else?"

"I'm glad you feel that way, but there *is* something else. I want you to come with me. To meet my family. To see where I grew up. I'm crazy about you, and it's important to me that you see my roots, or I don't think you'll ever really know me or understand me." He seemed to hesitate before he plunged ahead. "What you said about acting weird and changing . . . you need to know that if you come, I may seem . . . different from what you're used to. I'll be dressing in my Amish clothing for the wedding, as that'll be expected, and maybe other times as well. There's also a good chance I'll fall back into some of the dialect . . . the Amish are rooted in old German and still use some of their language, but they put out an effort to not speak it much around strangers who don't understand."

"Oh. I see. I think I'd like to come. Sure." She tried to smile again, but she didn't see. Not at all. And part of her was terrified she'd never understand, and that this return to his old life would mean an end to their new one.

Chapter Four

FIVE DAYS LATER, APRIL TUCKED A modest dress into her open suitcase that lay on her bed while her sister watched, the silence growing between them. She'd told May all about her conversation with Jesse, but even now, April was still trying to take it all in.

"Amish. I'm still having trouble believing it." May scooted up against the headboard and cradled a pillow against her abdomen.

April tried to muster a smile. Somehow, she had to make this at least feel less unreal. "It's not that weird. I mean, they've settled all over in different states now. Pennsylvania, Ohio, Kentucky, I've even heard some families have traveled to Montana."

"But no electricity. No phones. They don't even drive cars. In the twenty-first century. That's unbelievable. No telling what else they do without."

"People all over the world grow up without phones or electricity. Or cars."

May rolled her eyes. "But not here in the U.S. He's from Pennsylvania, not Transylvania."

April shot her a glance that she hoped May would interpret as "time to stop."

"Sorry, sis. I guess he could have been hiding a lot worse than a buggy instead of a car and wearing a hat all the time."

April sank down onto the bed next to her suitcase. "I don't know if I can do this, May." There. She'd finally admitted it to someone besides herself. This whole meet-the-family-but-hey-they're-Amish, thing was a lot for her to swallow.

"What? Why not? You're going to meet his family, not join the Amish, for goodness sake."

"I know, but I don't have a clue about anything Amish. Other than what I've already said about the things they don't use. I don't know their customs or even how to behave around them. We're leaving tomorrow morning. What if they . . .?"

"If they what? Hate you? I guess you run that risk anytime you meet a boyfriend's family."

"Yeah, I get that, but what if they judge me *and* don't like me?"

"Ha. I know what that's like. So does Rob.

You know how hard it was when I brought him home. A black guy getting engaged to a very blond white girl." She hugged the pillow tighter as though for comfort at some of the returning memories. "Thankfully, both of our families are cool with it now, but not everyone was. This wouldn't be the first time you'll have to help someone accept a person with a different background. Not saying it's the same thing, but you have a good heart, April. So does Jesse. His family will see that. They'll see who you are inside. I'm sure of it."

"Thanks. I appreciate that. I wish I had more time. I could have read a few books about the Amish, so I'd at least feel more prepared." She folded a skirt and laid it on top of the other pile of clothing.

"I'm sure Jesse will fill you in on the drive there. I might be able to help too." She reached past April and pulled out a short skirt and sleeveless blouse and placed them on a chair by the bed. "I do know that the Amish don't show much bare skin. I'd go with dresses or maybe . . . skirts. At the worst, slacks and short sleeve blouses. No tank tops or anything short in the way of skirts. Think modest."

"Huh! What makes you such an expert?"

April folded her arms across her chest as she stared at her sister, not liking the prospect of no jeans or shorts. It wasn't exactly winter sweater weather, it was fall, but the temperatures were still warm.

"Rob and I spent a weekend in Lancaster a couple of years ago. We fell in love with the place. I noticed the way the women dress, and even the men. Very conservative, at best. They have their quirks that you have to get used to, but most of the ones I met were very nice people. Some are reserved and don't seem to trust outsiders, and they're a tight-knit community, although a few I met were helpful and sweet."

"Maybe you could recommend a place for me to stay then? Jesse said his family's home isn't large. He'll be rooming with his brother. He suggested I could bunk with his teenage sister, but I don't think I'm quite up for that."

May tossed the pillow to the side and beamed. "I have just the spot. We stayed at this cute B&B. The owner and I have stayed in touch. I'll text her and see if she has a room, and if not, if she can recommend somewhere to say." She pulled her phone out of her pocket and started punching in a message. Two minutes later, a ping sounded on her phone.

May read it and grinned. "Tabby said she'd love to have you. She's holding a room and will text you the address and room number. I gave her your cell number." May grinned. "Don't look so scared. You're going to have so much fun up there. You'll love it. I promise!"

April pulled open a dresser drawer, hoping to find something else that was presentable. Love was a strong word. Right now, she'd settle for not crashing and burning in front of Jesse's family. She'd never been afraid of new experiences, but this one definitely had her rattled.

"Wow!" April twisted her head to see out the car window as Jesse drove through rolling hills and endless pastures of Amish country. "Slow down, would you?" She pointed up ahead. "I see a horse and buggy. I assume they're Amish, right? Beautiful." She breathed the word, not waiting for Jesse's reply as he slowed the car and moved to the center of the road to pass the black buggy with the single horse pulling it. She craned to see the driver as they passed, but all she caught a glimpse of was a black hat and clothing and a whip extending out over the horse's back.

Jesse chuckled. "I grew up riding in those, so I guess I forget what it must be like for someone new to see one for the first time. Pretty cool, *ya*?"

She swiveled to meet his gaze. "Ya? What was that?"

Color rose up into his cheeks. "Sorry. My family roots seem to be cropping up the closer we get to home. That's Amish for yes. You'll also hear goot for good, maam and *daed* for mom and dad, *Gott* for God, and a few others that are similar to English, but different. It goes back to what's called Pennsylvania Dutch, which has its roots in old Germanic."

"I see. I kind of like it. Maybe I'll pick up a few new words while we're there. That is, if it doesn't offend anyone? I don't want to do that."

He shook his head and tossed her a smile. "As long as you're being respectful, no one will mind." He slowed the car and put on his blinker. "We're going to make a quick stop. I thought we might buy a pie for mom." He grinned. "Or maam, as she prefers being called." They came to a stop a few feet from a charming sign that appeared to be hand painted that read Welcome to A Bird in Hand General Store.

"Quaint. I like it." April pushed open her door and stepped out, looking around. The front of the store fronting the sidewalk had tables loaded with fresh produce, and the double door stood open, allowing an amazing aroma to waft out, making April's mouth water. "What do I smell? Fresh baked goods? Yum!" She slipped her hand through Jesse's arm and allowed him to lead her inside, excited to see what the small store had to offer. She pulled out a shopping cart from behind the front door. Spotting a table loaded with pies, she released Jesse, then rushed over to the table. "No way are we only getting one pie. What's this one?" She pointed at something that looked something like chocolate hamburger buns with white whipped frosting in the middle.

Jesse draped his arm around her shoulders. "That's a whoopie pie. They are spectacular."

April put two of them into her basket. "These are coming with me." She picked up a square yellow bar sprinkled with confectioners' sugar and held it up for Jesse to see.

"Lemon bar. My mouth is watering looking at it."

She sighed. "Another keeper. I'm going to gain ten pounds on this trip." She placed the wrapped treat into her basket alongside the whoopie pies.

A young Amish man strolled by, stopped, and tipped his hat. "Jesse. Goot to see you." He nodded at April. "*Gutten-morgen.*"

She barely kept her mouth from gaping but managed to smile when she figured out what he'd said. "Good morning to you, too."

Jesse reached out a hand which the other man grasped. "Leroy. Nice to see you as well. This is April, my girlfriend."

The man gave her a solemn smile. "You've come for your brudder's wedding, ya?"

"Ya." Jesse nodded. "I wouldn't have missed it."

"Then I'll see you again." He moved on down the aisle, seemingly intent on whatever brought him into the store.

April moved around the large table until she stood in front of a wonderous assortment of pies. "Apple. Marionberry. Rhubarb. Cherry."

She gazed at Jesse, wondering how they'd ever choose. "I want all of them."

He laughed as he moved up beside her. "If you want a true Amish pie, you need to start with shoofly."

"Ugh. That sounds—awful. It doesn't have flies in it, does it?" She barely repressed a shudder.

"No, silly. It's made with molasses, brown sugar and eggs. But I can see why you'd think that from the name." He picked up one and carried it to the counter. Then he snagged a rhubarb, and April followed with a marionberry of her own.

The Amish woman nodded as she began totaling their purchases on what looked to be an antique cash register, large and covered with a lot of brass. "I haven't seen you in a while, Jesse Hardin."

"I'm here for Levi's wedding—and your pies, of course, Mrs. Samuels."

The woman smiled and gave him the total as she began boxing the pies.

A middle-aged Amish man strode through the door and waved. "Jesse. How are you, young man?"

Jesse waved in return then pulled his

wallet from his back pocket as the man headed down an aisle in the opposite direction.

April leaned close. "You seem to know everyone around here."

"Not everyone, but it is a small town and a tight-knit community. I'm sure there are a few new people who've moved here since I left." He picked up the stack of pie boxes while April took the bag with the pastries. "*Bis schpeeder*, Mrs. Samuels."

She nodded and smiled as they walked to the door.

April waited until they'd gone through the door out of earshot. "What did that mean?"

"It means, see you later in Pennsylvania Dutch."

She raised her brows, hit even more with the realization that this world was not only different from what she was used to, but completely foreign. "Anything else I need to know?"

They loaded their items in the backseat of the car, climbed in, and buckled their seat belts. Jesse seemed to be thinking as they pulled back onto the road. "Well, since you asked, there are a few things. Like, the Amish don't listen to music. They've never heard of

Louis Armstrong, Elvis Presley—"

"Beyoncé?" April turned to face him. "I had no idea. I guess I should have figured that out since they don't use electricity."

"Exactly. So don't get your heart set to dancing at the wedding. On the plus side, there's going to be a lot of great food."

"Right. What else?"

Jesse turned onto a gravel driveway that had a few bumps and ridges.

April clutched the door handle as he navigated a bit of a rough spot. "They don't pave their driveways either?"

He grinned. "You nailed it."

They both gazed out over the pastures alongside the driveway, dotted with horses and a couple of cows. The fence appeared in need of repairs and a modest, two-story house stood at the end of the lane, with a red, two-story barn just beyond. "This is your home?"

Jesse looked at the house, the barn, and the work that had been neglected on the fence, wondering why his brother hadn't done more to keep it in repair. He'd need to lend Levi a hand while they were here and see if he could make a difference. He almost itched to get his hands on a hammer and replace the broken rail he'd seen on the wood fence back near the road.

"Jesse?" April broke into his thoughts.

He came to a stop and put the car in park while still a ways from the house, taking it all in, loathe to rush there while memories surged. "Sorry. Yes. This is home. Or it used to be, years ago. It was the center of my world. Working the farm, going to church, spending time with my brother and then my baby sister when she came along, helping Daed with the chores." He shot April a glance. "Life was so much simpler then. We read by lantern light. Got up at the crack of dawn and never ate out—Maam is an amazing cook, and no one would ever consider paying someone else to cook a meal."

April smiled. "I can't imagine you with a big hat and a long beard."

Jesse laughed. "I did wear a hat, but only married men grow beards. You should have seen my daed's beard. It was amazing." He sighed. "I guess we should get moving." He put the car back into gear and crept forward, navigating around another bump. "I can't believe how bad this road has gotten. Daed always kept it up. I need to have a talk with Levi."

"I'm guessing he's had his hands full getting ready for his wedding."

Jesse grunted. "You may be surprised. This isn't like any wedding you've ever attended, April. No white gown or tuxes or music playing. Very simple and . . . plain."

All of a sudden, the car lurched, and a soft pop and a hiss sounded from the right front tire.

April jerked upright. "What was that? Did we hit something?"

Jesse pulled the car to the side, and they got out and walked to the front of the car. A broken fence post lay just behind the front wheel of a quickly deflating tire. "What in the world? Why would a fence post be out here?"

"Great question. It has a nail sticking out of it, which is what punctured our tire."

April placed her hands on her hips. "Do we have a spare?"

"I'm sure we do. I'll take a look." He opened the driver's side door and reached in to pop the trunk. He walked back and raised it the rest of the way, sticking his head inside to check for the tire.

"You Englischers get lost?" A man spoke

behind them and made Jesse jerk his head upright. He cracked it on the rim of the trunk. "Ouch!" He rubbed his head and turned to see his grinning, clean-shaven brother walking toward them. Jesse took two big strides forward, grasped Levi's hand, and then slapped him on the back a couple of times for good measure. "Levi. Great to see you." He turned and gestured toward the fence post under the car. "You responsible for this booby trap?"

Levi heaved a soft sigh. "It's on my list of things to do. I knew I'd missed something. There's a lot to do here since Daed died. Sorry, brudder."

Jesse motioned April over. "Levi, this is April, my girlfriend."

April smiled, her face lighting as she shook Levi's hand. "Hello. It's so nice to meet you."

"Hello, April the girlfriend. Pleased to meet you as well and honored you could come to my wedding."

"Thank you. I'm very honored you allowed me to come. You and Sarah must be so excited."

"Yes, ma'am. We're both looking forward to it."

"Jesse!" A young girl with hints of red in her hair dashed toward them. April thought she spotted a hint of deviltry in those eyes and that grin, and she definitely wasn't acting like a proper young Amish woman the way she dashed toward them. Fifteen, maybe sixteen? She appeared to be a handful. She launched herself at Jesse, nearly knocking him over.

Jesse laughed and struggled to regain his footing. "Whoa, there, Rachel. It's great to see you too, but leave me standing, if you please." He gripped her by her shoulders and took a step back. "My. You're almost grown up. April, meet my baby sister, Rachel." He gave the girl one more quick hug and then released her. "Where did my baby sister go since I've been gone?"

Rachel huffed. "Younger sister, not baby sister. I'm sixteen now." She reached out and shook April's hand. Her grip was soft but firm, giving April an impression of hidden strength mixed with femininity. She wore a simple dark blue dress with long sleeves and a skirt to her calves, along with a white capp with the strings untied. A little of her auburn hair peeked out under the capp, but most of it was pulled back into a bun at the base of her neck.

April liked this girl, as she'd liked Levi the

moment she met him. Maybe this meeting-the-family gig wouldn't be so bad, after all. Hopefully, their mother would be as warm and welcoming as these two, and she'd be home-free and able to relax. "We picked up a few sweets along the way. Maybe you can help me eat one of these whoopie pies." She reached into the car and pulled out the bag of bakery goodies.

Rachel's face fell. "Nothing from New York City? I was hoping for a bagel or a pizza. A friend told me they make amazing ones there."

April tipped her head to the side. "New York City?"

"Not this time, Rachel, sorry." Jesse reached in and grabbed the boxes of pies and handed one to Levi.

He took it and nodded at Rachel. "She's just beginning her Rumspringa. She's very curious about the Englisch lately."

Rachel huffed. "So what if I am? There's nothing wrong with that."

April tried to hide her smile. This teen was nothing if not feisty. She was guessing the two of them might become friends.

Jesse held up one hand. "Easy, *schwester*. It's fine if you want to learn more about the

Englisch world, but there are many things here at home you would miss if you left. Believe me. I know."

Rachel narrowed her eyes but didn't smile. "Fine. If you say so. But as I remember, you still left."

"Rachel, why don't you take April inside while Jesse and I tend to this car." Levi stepped around to the open trunk. "You have a spare tire?"

Jesse joined him but reached up to close the trunk. "It'll be fine for a while. I want to see Maam first. She'll wonder if I don't come in."

Levi gave a slow nod. "Yes, well . . . do not expect the warmest of welcomes."

Rachel bounced on her toes next to April. "Ya. She's still upset about you and Naomi Trotter."

April bit her lip. "Uh . . . Naomi Trotter?" Her heartbeat increased as she looked at the warmth suffusing Jesse's cheeks. Was there a girlfriend here that he'd left behind and hadn't told her about? One his mother was still hoping he'd marry?

Jesse reached out and squeezed her arm. "Nothing to worry about. Just a girl I grew up with. We were in the same class and played together as kids. Amish mothers pride themselves on their matchmaking skills, and while I was still at home and a young boy, Maam picked Naomi for me. But Naomi is married now, so it doesn't matter." He tossed a look at April. "Happily married, I might add." He started walking toward the house with April at his side.

Rachel popped up next to them. "No. She's not, Jesse. She's probably going to be looking for a husband again soon. Hers passed away well over a year ago."

Jesse nearly came to a halt, causing April to stumble. "Oh. I'm sorry to hear that."

April's heart crashed. Not nearly as sorry as she felt she was apt to be from the way it sounded.

Rachel hefted one of the pie boxes. "There's rhubarb in here?"

April nodded but couldn't bring herself to reply.

"Goot. When Maam sees it, she'll forget all about Naomi. Guaranteed."

April's steps lagged, and she let Jesse bound up the steps without her. What had she gotten herself into?

Chapter Five

Jesse walked into the kitchen of the farmhouse, reveling in the sights, sounds, and smells that brought back so many good—and even a few not-so-great—memories. He couldn't credit what Levi and Rachel told him about Maam still pining after Naomi to be his wife. Too many years had passed, and no doubt, Naomi was still grieving the loss of her husband.

Maam had her back to him as he entered, and he moved to a corner of the room quietly and watched her for a moment. Her hair that was once brown was now liberally sprinkled with gray. Esther Hardin's shoulders sagged, as though she carried a weight too great to bear, and she'd put on a bit of weight. All-in-all, her appearance, at least from the back, startled him. "Maam? I'm home." His voice came out softer and more tentative than he'd planned. She didn't turn, and he couldn't be sure she'd heard him. Why didn't he rush forward and envelope her in a hug like he used to do as a child? Then he remembered the resentment he'd seen flash across her face more than one time since he'd made the decisions not to join the church and to leave home. Hugs might not be in his future until she forgave him that decision.

Rachel and Levi came in behind him, with Rachel chattering non-stop to April. A pang of guilt hit him. He should have walked in with April, not rushed ahead and forgotten her.

Maam spun around, her eyes going straight to his sister. "There you are, Rachel. You were gone too long. I need you to start on the cabbage rolls."

"You said I could take a break." Rachel's face dissolved into something as close to a scowl as their mother would permit without serious consequences.

"Ya, I did, and you did. Now it's time for work." She eyed the box Rachel held. "What is that?" She pointed, took the box from Rachel's hands, and then opened it.

"Rhubarb pie, Maam." Levi moved up beside his mother. "From—"

"Jesse Hardin." Jesse moved from the darkened corner and stepped next to April.

"And from April. You didn't expect us to show up emptyhanded, did you?"

Maam didn't so much as glance at April but kept her stony expression on him. "I never know what to expect from you, boy."

Levi raised a hand. "I have a fence to mend. I'll be back later for supper." He exited the room but shot a glance back at Jesse that seemed to contain sympathy.

Jesse waited while his mother examined him from the top of his head to his shined shoes. "You are too thin. I'm glad you've come back to get some real food in your belly. Maybe I can fatten you up while you're here." Her gaze turned toward April and her brows rose, but her lips only thinned into a flat line.

"Maam, this is April Monroe, my girlfriend. I told Levi I'd be bringing her. April, this is my mother, Esther Hardin."

Esther squared her shoulders. "It's Mrs. Hardin."

April smiled. "It's a pleasure to meet you, Mrs. Hardin. You have a lovely home. It's so nice to be here."

"Not lovely yet. There's still too much work to do. I've been working day and night trying to get it all done with a little help from Rachel and

Levi, when they aren't dreaming about Englischers or getting married." She sniffed and turned her head. "My joints have been hurting all week, so I'm not moving as fast as I need to. Rachel—wash those first!"

Rachel looked up from starting to peel the outer leaves off the cabbage. "Yes, Maam." She walked to the sink and turned on the water.

Her response sounded more than a little begrudging to Jesse. It appeared his little sister's Rumspringa might be more of a challenge than his had been. He inwardly winced at what that could mean for his family—especially his mother. She'd taken it every bit as hard as his father had when he'd decided to leave the Amish community, and nothing had been the same since.

His maam walked back to the stove and stirred a pot with something in it that was bubbling. An amazing aroma wafted up, making his mouth water. He'd been telling the truth when he told April that Maam was a wonderful cook. He hadn't realized how much he'd missed her cooking and home.

April moved to her side. "What are you making?"

Maam plopped the lid back on the pot.

"You'll find out soon enough at supper. Besides, I imagine my son hasn't taught you much about Amish cooking."

"No, but he did tell me all about rhubarb pie and shoofly pie. I've never had either, but they sound good."

She whirled toward April and gave a mirthless laugh. "What kind of woman has never had rhubarb pie? I can understand shoofly pie, as that's mostly a dish we make, but rhubarb?" She planted her arms over her chest and glared.

Jesse stepped forward. "Maam."

She looked at him and then glanced at April. "I apologize. But you must have many more worldly pleasures in New York that keep you busy since cooking doesn't seem to be one of your gifts."

April had all she could do to keep from gasping. What was with this woman? She acted as though she'd taken an instant dislike to her the minute she walked through the door. Then she remembered. Naomi Trotter. Of course. Mrs. Hardin resented the fact that Jesse was dating a . . . what did they call outsiders? Englischer. Great. This was going to make for a very pleasant visit. "Actually, Mrs. Hardin, I enjoy trying new things, and I'm sure I'll love it. I've dabbled at cooking off and on, although I'm sure I'm not as accomplished as you are."

Mrs. Hardin sniffed. "I'm sure."

April gave Jesse a look that she hoped he'd interpret as needing his help.

He stepped forward and put his arm around her shoulders. His mother's brows drew down in a deeper frown. "Since you're busy, I think I'll give April a tour of the house and the farm. Unless you need help, Maam?"

She snorted another laugh, her dripping spoon held up. "*Nein*. No help. But she's not staying here, is she? We are already completely full. There is no room, and she cannot stay with you in your room." She glared at April so hard she wanted to take a step back.

"No, Mrs. Hardin. I have a room at a bed and breakfast in town. The Sunflower Inn. Jesse told me you'd have a full house, and I'd never think of staying with Jesse."

Mrs. Hardin nodded but didn't smile. "Goot. I would certainly hope not. Jesse has become worldly enough going into the Englisch world without a woman leading him further astray."

April hesitated and then drew in a quick breath. "I'm happy to stay and help you with supper. The tour can wait, I'm sure. I'm pretty good with my hands."

Mrs. Hardin smirked. "Of course, you are."

Jesse drew April closer. "Maam, April is a doctor."

Rachel whirled around and clapped her hands. "That's awesome!"

"Rachel." Mrs. Hardin quenched Rachel's excitement with that one word. "What have I told you about using Englischer slang? It is not allowed in this house even if you are on your Rumspringa."

April could tell from Rachel's expression that she'd roll her eyes if she thought she could get away with it. Then her face sobered to something beyond believable, and she gave a small bow. "I apologize, Maam. April, your chosen profession is exceedingly commendable."

April almost laughed but caught it when she saw the hard gleam in Mrs. Hardin's eyes. "Umm. Thank you."

Mrs. Hardin placed the dripping spoon

back in the pot. "Thank you, April. We don't need any help. We can manage supper on our own. But should I cut myself, you'll be the first one I call, I'm sure."

April and Jesse headed for the front door, and April waited until they were out of earshot. "She seems . . . a bit upset? I mean, I guess, maybe it was a shock meeting me. . ."

Jesse wrapped her in a tight hug. "She'll come around. It's impossible not to fall in love with you. I think Rachel and Levi are already on your side."

"Even if I've never had rhubarb pie?"

He grinned. "Nobody's perfect."

She slugged him in the arm, but somehow, her heart felt a little lighter.

Esther Hardin stirred the bubbling pot for all she was worth, doing her best not to let tears drip into the liquid. What was wrong with her boy, bringing an outsider among them? Wasn't it enough that he'd left their people, their faith, their community? Did he have to bring a stranger here as well? She'd set her heart on him marrying Naomi years ago. Then Naomi had found another and married. Now that she was free again, she'd so hoped that Jesse would come to his senses and court her again. Maybe then he'd move home. She sighed. She'd seen how her boy looked at that Englischer, but maybe all was not lost. When he saw Naomi again at the wedding, she prayed the old interest would be fanned into life again. Naomi had asked about his arrival and what he was doing now, and she'd seen a gleam in the younger woman's eyes whenever Jesse's name was mentioned.

"Maam?" Rachel touched her arm, and she jumped.

"What is it? Are you finished preparing the cabbage yet? If so, you need to set the table." She shooed her away. So much to still get done for this wedding, and now another mouth to feed and not even one who understood their ways. What was Jesse thinking?

Rachel didn't move. "I spoke to you three times, and you didn't answer. Are you all right?"

"Of course, I am. What a silly girl, always thinking things that aren't real. You need to get your head out of the clouds, child, and back on your chores and family where it belongs."

Rachel bit her lip and waited a moment

before she replied. "Yes, Maam. What did you think of April? She seems very sweet."

"Humph. Sweet is as sweet does. She hasn't proven herself yet, so we shall see. Now go set the table. Your brothers will be back in soon looking for supper."

"My brothers and April, Maam. Not just Levi and Jesse." Rachel walked backward toward the dining area. "I don't see what you have against her. She was very polite, and she's a doctor. Jesse is a doctor as well, even if it's for animals, so they probably have a lot in common."

Fear reared its head and roared through Esther's mind. Her son was smitten with this Englischer, and now her daughter was as well? Wasn't it enough that she'd lost her husband and was alone with only one of her children who might choose to continue in the Amish way? What would become of her if Rachel left as well. She would have to do everything in her power to make sure that didn't happen—and everything in her power to show Jesse he'd made a mistake and that coming home and settling down with a quiet Amish woman was for the best. That Englisch woman might be nice enough—she had been polite and not loud or intrusive, she'd give her that—but she wasn't Amish, and she'd never fit in. Dread filled Esther at the possibility that she might lose most of her family. If that happened, she didn't know how she could go on.

Jesse stopped by his old room with April, making that the last one on the house tour. "This was my room, what feels now like many years ago. Simple, plain, but comfortable."

April ran her hand over the squares of the quilt his mother had made him when he turned twelve. "It's lovely. The quilt and the furniture."

"Ya. There's nothing like Amish furniture. We have some of the best craftsmen in the world, for sure and for certain."

She raised her brows at him and grinned. "More Pennsylvania Dutch?" She was glad they'd left the kitchen and the cranky woman who obviously disliked her. She'd never met such open hostility from someone before—well, other than Dr. Schneider, of course. Maybe by the time they came in for supper, Mrs. Hardin would have come to accept that April wasn't a threat.

He laughed. "That is a rather common expression, I'm afraid. I guess I'm falling back into it faster than I expected."

"It's okay. Like I said, it's nice." She walked over to the window. "What a view. It's amazing here." She looked out across the grassy fields dotted with cows and a couple of horses, the barn not far from the house and large oak and maple trees giving shade. She thought she saw a hint of a stream in the distance not far from the barn. Lovely. So peaceful and quiet here—nothing at all like New York. She could get used to this kind of peace.

He moved up beside her. "Yes, there's nothing quite like it—but it'll be more fun exploring outside, not just looking at it. Come on." He grabbed her hand and pulled her toward the door.

They strolled hand-in-hand toward the huge barn, and April raised her eyes all the way to the top where a weathervane sat. "Do the Amish really have barn raisings? Or was that something that only happened in the old west a hundred years or so ago?"

"No, it happens here too. If someone's barn burns down or any kind of tragedy strikes, the community gets together en-masse. They can put a simple one up in a day. This one, however, took us four days, as it has a large loft, milking and horse stalls, a tack room, and a spot for separating the milk."

April's mouth gaped open. "You built a barn?"

He laughed. "I was pretty young at the time, so I held nails for my dad and lugged roof shingles over one at a time. I was only six, so I wasn't a lot of help, but I tried. Of course, Daed told me how proud he was of my help and how they couldn't have done it without me. I believed him until I got old enough to realize how young I'd been . . . and that I'd probably been in the way more than a help." His smile sobered. "I miss him."

April squeezed his hand. "Yeah, I get that. I felt the same way when my grandpa died. It's so hard losing someone you love. The only thing that helped was knowing I'd see him again in Heaven."

Jesse nodded but didn't reply. He drew her along beside him as they crossed a small meadow and came to the bank of a slow-moving brook. "This is the property line on one side of our place. Hardin Brook. If you look closely, you can see trout occasionally. Daed and I used to try to catch fish for supper, but it didn't happen very often. I always felt sorry for the fish when we did catch them. I never was able to kill one."

April smiled. "A born animal lover. I can totally see you being that way."

He heaved a big sigh. "Daed never really understood me . . . and I guess I didn't really understand him, either. I loved him, of course, but we were at odds pretty often. He wanted me to be a farmer, like him. Or at least go into woodworking and make furniture. Anything that was traditional Amish and would keep me here on the farm. I tried to fit in, really I did." He shook his head and stared at the water.

April slipped her hand through his arm and hugged it against her side, hoping to convey how much she cared and understood. There was so much to this man—depths she hadn't begun to plumb, and she yearned to see more facets of his personality that were only now beginning to reveal themselves.

"Let's sit on the grass for a few minutes. I really want time with you to myself before we have to go face the family again," Jesse said. They sank onto the large patch of grass near the water. "It's so strange being back here without Daed around. I always hoped we'd be able to make up—that we'd find a way to have peace between us—some kind of neutral ground, I guess. But it didn't happen. He died before we had the chance to do that. I still miss him. I still hope Maam and I can find a way to reach that middle ground and discover a place of respect, if not understanding."

April leaned into him. "I think you will. Your heart is in the right place. You love your family, and it shows."

"Thanks." He looked up at her. "Our families are so different. It's probably hard for you to understand. Your family all get along. There's no tension like there is in there." He waved toward the house. "I'm so sorry Maam treated you that way. Amish are normally very polite. Reserved at times, yes, but hospitable and not . . . unkind. I think she's still dealing with me not being home."

"I appreciate that, but I'm guessing you're right. It's hard for her to have a son leave his way of life and then bring a girlfriend home who's an outsider." As the words left her mouth, April realized she did understand. She couldn't imagine what that might be like for Jesse's mother. Maybe she could find ways to make it easier for Mrs. Hardin to accept her while they were here. "But my family has had their share of hard times, too."

He cocked one brow. "Not from what I've seen. All of you seem to love each other."

April gave him a rueful smile. "Rob and May got engaged in college, and none of the parents approved. And I mean none. They felt they were too young and coming from such 'different cultures and families.' My parents' words. Rob's parents had their own set of objections, none of which Rob or May appreciated or agreed with."

Jesse held up his hand, palm out. "Hold it. From what I've seen, your parents love Rob. This is just weird."

"Right. They do now, several years later, but it took time and getting to know him . . . and his family getting acquainted with May, before they started to open their minds and apologize. Thankfully, Rob and May had the grace and ability to accept those apologies and give them another chance, but it could have gone very differently."

Jesse shook his head. "I had no idea."

April shrugged. "There are some things in my past that I don't choose to talk about, and that's one of them. The hurt ran deep for several years, and I was caught in the middle. I loved my parents, but I didn't agree with their behavior, and I hurt for May. It's a blessing those times are all behind us now. That was another thing that brought both families around. May and Rob sat them down individually and asked them if this is what Christian love and acceptance looks like, and it stunned them. That was the turning point." She waved her hand in the air. "What I'm trying to say is, if my family could make it through that, I think your family will find a way to reconcile as well."

Chapter Six

Jesse knew he'd need to spend time mulling over what April had told him. She had a lot of wisdom, and he was thankful she'd shared about her family. He struggled with the idea that his maam would ever come around, and with Daed already gone . . . well, that was water under the bridge. He was going to have to try to deal with his mother one way or the other.

They walked back toward the house by way of the large vegetable garden just beyond the barn, a handy location for organic fertilizer. Jesse tried not to laugh. How many big-city people would be horrified if they realized exactly where the fertilizer came from that made their lush fruits and vegetables.

As they approached, Levi stood and placed his hand at the small of his back and groaned. "Could you two help harvest the celery? Maam needs it straight away."

"At your service, little brudder." Jesse rolled up his sleeves, grabbed a stalk, and then twisted it off its base. He tossed the first one into the wooden basket with the ones Levi had already harvested. April watched for a moment and then bent to try her hand at it. Jesse would guess this was the first time she'd done anything like this, and he rather enjoyed the sight of her working beside him. He'd grown up doing this kind of thing, and it brought back good memories. At least, most of them were good. "Not bad, April. Next thing you know, we'll have you up at 5:00 a.m. to help milk the cows."

She stood and tossed a stalk in. "What's all the celery for? It seems like an awful lot."

"Creamed celery. It's traditional at weddings. You know, like mashed potatoes at Thanksgiving."

Levi straightened as well. "But more delicious."

Jesse shook dirt from the bunch he held before throwing it in. "An abundant celery garden can be one way to tell when a wedding is coming up. Amish couples are very secretive about their plans, which is why this one didn't write to me until the last minute."

Levi scowled. "You know I've never been one to break tradition—hey!" He ducked as a dirt clod sailed toward him. He picked one up and threw it back at Jesse, but it almost hit April.

April dodged to the side. "Watch out there, boys. Some of us didn't grow up taking part in dirt fights."

"Sorry, April." Levi dusted off his hands. "You know, it's kind of nice working outside. I like this. It might even be worth it getting these new jeans dirty."

"Jesse!" Rachel ran toward them, waving her hands. "Maam says to bring what you have. We need to get ready for supper. She invited Sarah and her family and a couple of other people, and I've already set the table."

"Already? I didn't have a chance to help. I'm sorry." April looked from Rachel to Jesse.

Rachel shook her head. "Maam's just in a mood because of the wedding coming up. Please don't take it personally."

Jesse grabbed April's hand and pulled her toward the house, hoping his little sister was right, but fearing it was far more than that. "Ya. Amish eat pretty early since we go to bed early. Nothing like the eight o'clock dinners in New York. We'd never get any work done if we stayed up late. I wasn't kidding about the 5:00 a.m. milking. Come on. We need to get cleaned up and ready to eat."

April watched the people moving from the dining room to the expansive kitchen and worried her bottom lip as she boiled a pot of sauce on the stove. All of the men wore dark suits with white shirts, and many of the women were dressed in plain, simple dresses with white capps and aprons. She glanced down at her aqua-marine dress with the lace at the cuffs and neck and then turned to Jesse. "I should have worn something more . . ."

Jesse squeezed her hand. "Amish?"

"I feel out of place. Like a peacock among the hens." She placed her free hand over her mouth. "I'm so sorry. I didn't mean that the way it came out. I was referring to the colors, that's all."

Jesse gave her hand another quick squeeze, and laughter filled his eyes. "You look wonderful, or *wunderbar*, as Levi would say. If it wouldn't scandalize everyone here, I'd kiss you right now."

She whooshed out a soft breath and tried to relax. "Thank you. That's sweet. Levi's fianceé Sarah is very quiet, but she seems nice." She tipped her head at the young redheaded woman standing beside Levi, just visible through the large archway leading from the kitchen into the living area.

Levi moved forward to answer a rap at the front door, Sarah at his side.

"I agree." Jesse kept his attention on the door. "I wonder who's here now? I thought everyone had come."

An older Amish man entered and shook Levi's hand and then gave a small bow to Sarah. "A blessing to see you, Sarah."

"Mr. Trotter, how good of you to come." Her musical, low voice barely reached April's ears, but she perked up at the name Trotter. Could this be a relative of the infamous Naomi whom Mrs. Hardin had set her heart on marrying Jesse?

"We didn't realize you'd be coming, Daniel." Levi ushered the man in.

"Your mother didn't tell you? Although we only received her invitation yesterday."

"We?" Levi's forehead crinkled, and dread hit April square in the middle.

A stunning young Amish woman with a blonde wave of hair escaping from under the forehead of her capp entered behind Mr. Trotter and slipped her hand through his arm. "Papa, I wasn't able to carry both boxes." She smiled at Levi. "We brought fresh pies I baked today, in your and Sarah's honor—and to welcome back the prodigal son. I heard he's here?" Her gaze swept the room until it landed on Jesse standing just inside the kitchen door. She shoved the boxed pie in her father's hands and rushed toward him. "Jesse!" She reached out as though to wrap him in a hug, but he extended his hand and grasped hers.

"Naomi. It's been a long time. I had no idea you were coming."

"Your maam invited us." She gave him a coy smile that almost made April wince, it was so bright. "She and I have always been close, and it's been wonderful to have her friendship, especially this past year." Her eyes lowered demurely.

Jesse didn't release his hold on her hand. "I was sorry to hear about your husband. That must have been hard."

She took a step closer and leaned her shoulder against Jesse's. "Thank you. He was a goot man." She turned to her father. "Papa, you remember Jesse?"

The man walked over, stroking his full beard. "Ah, yes, indeed. The young man who brought my daughter home from so many frolics?"

"Frolics?" April couldn't keep silent any longer and took a step toward Jesse.

He seemed to come to himself and dropped Naomi's hand. Then he reached out and put an arm around April's shoulders. "Naomi, this is April."

"His girlfriend." She extended her hand, noticing this was the first time Jesse hadn't introduced her that way. "Nice to meet you."

The other woman gave her a brief handshake that told April a little about her personality. Then she batted her eyes. "Mrs. Hardin has told me so much about you."

April gave a nervous laugh. "Well, none of it's true."

Naomi arched one brow, and a tiny smile tipped the corner of her lips. "Nein? I've always found Esther Hardin to be a reliable judge of character and never one to exaggerate or tell tales."

April's smile faded. "I was . . . joking."

"So? Then everything she said is true?"

"Naomi, Daniel!" Esther Hardin rushed into the room. "There you are. I'm so glad you arrived. I was beginning to worry you wouldn't make it." She smiled at Daniel and then gave Naomi a warm hug.

Daniel gave a brief bow, but a bashful smile flitted around his bewhiskered lips. "Esther. You are looking well tonight."

"*Danke.*"

Did April see a hint of color in the woman's cheeks? Could she be interested in this man who must be a widower? Wouldn't that put the cherry on the cake if the two of them got together. All one big happy family with Naomi right in the middle. Suddenly, the thought of eating supper soured April's stomach.

Esther beamed at Naomi. "I'm sorry to interrupt you and Jesse's chat, but I need someone who is useful in the kitchen, if you don't mind?"

Naomi shot a small smirk at April. "Of course, I'd be happy to help. I'll talk to you later, Jesse." Almost as an afterthought, she glanced at April. "You too, April."

Jesse sat across from April but next to Naomi, more than a little frustrated at his mother's seating plan at the table. It was obvious she was trying to push him toward his old girlfriend, but that had ended years ago, and he'd rarely thought of Naomi again. It hadn't even given him the tiniest pang of jealousy or sorrow when he'd heard she'd married. More a sense of relief that he'd escaped. Not that she wasn't a nice girl. She'd always been polite and respectful, and everything an Amish young woman should be, but she didn't send his heart into overdrive like April did. He smiled across the table at April, so proud of her, the way she worked to be kind to his mother and family. This had to be a hard situation for her.

Naomi's voice broke through his thoughts. "I swear, you were born hungry, Jesse Hardin. You always could eat as much as two men, even when you were a teen."

He smiled at her. "You can't find food like this in New York. Pass the creamed celery?" He reached for it as Naomi handed it to him, and her fingers brushed his, seeming to linger a moment. He glanced at April and saw her gaze riveted on Naomi's hand.

Sarah smiled at April. "Tell me about yourself, April. What do you do in the Englisch world?"

"I'm a doctor. A family doctor, general

practice, at a large hospital in New York." April returned her smile then took a drink of her water.

Sarah nodded. "That must be very rewarding work, helping people who are sick."

"Yes, it is, although at times it's difficult when a patient is really ill and I have to send them to a specialist, or I'm not able to help." Her serious expression changed to one of merriment. "Or when someone comes up to me at a dinner party wanting me to diagnose a rash or a cough." She giggled and looked around. "If any of you have a rash or a cough, though, I'd be happy to help."

Levi laughed with her. "I feel perfectly fine, but your offer is very much appreciated, April."

Jesse could have hugged his younger brother since more than one of the older people at the table seemed less than entertained. Frowns marred more than one face, and they shot looks at one another across the table.

Daniel Trotter clucked his tongue. "We Amish do not put much stock in modern medicine, Miss Monroe."

Jesse leaned back in his seat as he watched April's face cloud over at the slight rebuke in the older man's tone. "Some Amish. The older, more stubborn ones. There are Amish who are willing to see a doctor."

His maam frowned at him. "I've never been to a doctor in my life, and I've always been healthy. I don't imagine that will ever change. I do not trust Englischer medicine."

April's eyes rounded. "Didn't you say something earlier about your joints giving you pain?"

Silence fell over the room, and no one seemed to breathe. Jesse cleared his throat. "The leaves are turning colors now. So many reds and oranges. The wedding will be beautiful."

Maam didn't seem to hear him or chose to ignore it. "We have natural remedies for such things."

April smiled, but Jesse could see her heart wasn't in it. "If they aren't working, maybe a doctor could prescribe a better—"

Maam broke in. "We don't tell you Englischers how to live your lives. We're content to leave well enough alone and mind our own business. It would be nice if they'd return the favor." She hmphed and leaned back in her chair.

Rachel emitted a small groan. "Maam."

April sat as though stunned for a long moment. Then she pushed back her chair, the wooden legs scraping the floor and squeaking. "If you'll excuse me, please. Dinner was . . . wonderful. Thank you."

Jesse bolted from his chair. "April."

He glanced at Naomi and saw the remnants of a smirk that she quickly changed to a straight-lipped expression, but one brow rose as she met his gaze. Then he turned and glared at his mother. "You'll have to excuse me, as well." He stalked outside, hating the stunned expression he'd seen on April's face.

Esther watched the Englisher woman who was trying to take her Jesse away as she left the table with her son. Satisfaction warred with misery in Esther's chest. She'd seen the way her oldest boy had looked when she'd spoken harshly to the Englischer—like pain had smote him hard at her words. However, it was for the best. His brain was addled by her pretty appearance and by her probably sinful worldly ways. Her face burned at the thought, and she prayed he hadn't done anything for which to be ashamed. They'd always taught their children to respect the marriage vows and the marriage bed, but you could never be sure what they might do once they left the church.

If only her sweet Samuel hadn't died. Her husband would have known how to deal with this new situation. He'd always kept Jesse in line when he was a boy. She tried to push away the memories of her boy's sadness when Samuel had scolded him or not allowed him to keep the wounded bird he'd found and tried to help heal. Samuel had said it was foolish, but part of her had wanted to go to Jesse's defense. What trouble could one small bird cause for her boy who loved animals so much? But Samuel had put his foot down. Maybe he wouldn't be a help with Jesse now, but she'd have the comfort of his arms at night and a listening ear when she needed to talk. Right now, there was no one who understood the pain she felt at losing her husband and her son or the fear at the possibility that Rachel could be next.

Rachel was certainly no comfort. She was going the same way as Jesse. Ensnared by Englischer ways, that's what. Was she to lose all of her family except Levi? The thought worried her more than she liked to admit even to herself. Somehow, she must keep her family from leaving her. Find a way to win Jesse back home and get rid of that Englisch girl before she could put even more worldly notions into her Rachel's mind.

"Esther?" A light hand touched her arm and she started. "Yes? What?"

Naomi gave her a worried look. "Is everything all right?"

"Yes. It will be. Soon. You'll see." She took a bite of her pie and tried to muster a smile. Somehow, it had to be. She wasn't sure she could go on if it wasn't.

Chapter Seven

April stood outside the Hardin home hoping she could get a Lyft or Uber to pick her up, but she'd just gotten the message, "No drivers available," so she slid her phone back into her pocket. What had happened back there? Did Jesse's mother hate her that much, or had she stuck her foot in things by offering medical advice where it wasn't wanted? Or had Mrs. Hardin let the comment about her joints slip out earlier in the day and was now embarrassed that April had made a big deal of it in front of everyone else. Whatever the case, humiliation burned in her throat at the woman's rebuke. What would Jesse think? He was probably in there being regaled by the lovely Naomi.

Warm hands gripped her shoulders, and she jumped. "Oh, my." She whirled around to face Jesse's troubled gaze. "I'm sorry I made a hash of things in there. I should know not to try to give unsolicited medical advice."

He drew her into a close hug. "No. I'm sorry

for the way my mother treated you. It was uncalled for." He rubbed her back until she began to relax, some of the tension from moments before draining out of her body.

"I thought I might get a Lyft back to my room. I'm tired, and I think I'd like to go rest, but there are no drivers available."

He chuckled and took a half step back but still kept his arms loosely wrapped around her. "This is Amish country, remember?"

Her face crumpled. "I shouldn't have come, Jesse. I'm not wanted here. It would be better if I'd stayed in New York and you came on your own."

"Hey, slow down!" Jesse's head jerked a tiny bit as though in surprise. "Where's this coming from?"

She narrowed her eyes. "You *did* hear what went on in there, right? You saw the way your mother is trying to push Naomi at you? Honestly, the little comments about not being any help in the kitchen and not wanting advice from an Englischer—she's hoping to drive me away so she can marry you off to Naomi Trotter and get you to come back home."

"Probably." He tried to smile.

April gaped at him. "So you admit it?" She

pulled out of his embrace and took a few steps away, more than a little shocked and hurt. She thought he'd try to deny it and make excuses for his mother.

He stepped up beside her and touched her arm. "Look. Don't pay any attention to Maam."

April whirled on him. "But she hates me!"

Jesse shook his head. "I don't think so. She doesn't even know you, so how can she hate you? It means a lot to me that you want to make a good impression on my family and that you've been trying so hard. But if I cared that much what my mother thought, I never would have left the Amish life." He sighed. "Not that I don't care, I love her, but I didn't allow her to make life decisions for me then, and I'm not going to now. It's you I care about, April. Not what Maam wants and not Naomi Trotter."

Her heart melted and more of the worry and stress seemed to drain out. "You mean that? Truly?" She stepped into his arms and rested her head against his chest. She still had trouble dealing with all the innuendos and not-so-subtle hints from Mrs. Hardin, but she couldn't be happier with Jesse's assurances.

"Come on. Let's go back in."

She shook her head. "No. Not now,

anyway." She pulled away. "I need to check in at the B&B. They'll be expecting me. I'll feel more up to facing your family again tomorrow after a good night's sleep."

"If that's what you want."

"There's just one small problem. I think it's too far to walk, and the tire hasn't been replaced or fixed yet on the car."

Jesse gave her a sly grin. "I have the perfect ride for you, madame. Give me ten minutes, and I'll be at your service. Don't go anywhere."

April's heart sank as realization dawned. "No. No way, Jesse. Uh-uh. I'm a city girl, remember? I don't do horses and buggies." She watched him stride off without so much as looking back, but she knew he had to have heard what she said as he left. She'd had enough to deal with already. The thought of climbing into a rickety buggy and traveling the roads at night made her quake inside.

A few minutes later, April heard the soft *clip-clop* of hooves against the dirt drive before the buggy came into view with Jesse holding the reins. She shivered and rubbed her hands up and down her arms, not sure she was up to this new adventure. What if the horse ran away with them, or a car hit them, or . . .? She took a step back as the horse drew to a halt beside her and Jesse jumped out.

"Your ride awaits, my lady." He grinned and extended a hand. "I even took the time to get your luggage from the car and put it in the back." He waved at the black buggy, but with nothing but moonlight shining on it, April was hard-pressed to see where he indicated.

"O-kay." She kept her feet planted firmly on the ground where she knew she'd be safe. Somehow, this wasn't what she'd planned when she decided to stay in town at the B&B. "So . . . is this safe?"

This time Jesse laughed. "Yes, it's safe. I wouldn't still be here if not. It was my sole transportation growing up. Come on. Climb in." He cocked a brow at her. "Or do you need help?"

The last thing she wanted right now was to look like a sissy who couldn't even climb into a buggy on her own, but . . . "All right. Here goes." She grasped a handle on the side of the conveyance and stepped onto the small platform. Then she swung up and landed in the seat next to Jesse.

"Now that wasn't so bad, was it?" He tipped his head toward the bar with the narrow grate beneath it next to her right hip. "You can hold onto that if you get nervous. This is Maam's surrey. She has a fully enclosed buggy that we can let the canvas sides down on when it's raining or snowing. Thankfully, the weather is still warm and dry enough we don't need that one tonight."

She pulled her jacket closer around her. "It doesn't have a heater, right?"

"Right." He flipped the reins and clucked to the horse. "Giddap, Martha."

"Martha? For a horse? Really?" She clutched the metal railing as the buggy rolled forward.

"Yep. Maam likes to name them after ancestors that she liked. This one is a favorite great aunt, who I don't remember, but I'm sure she was nice, since the mare is. You doing all right over there?"

"So far so good, but what happens when we're not on your driveway and a car goes by?" She grabbed the rail again as the buggy wheels bounced through a small hole Levi must have missed filling earlier today. "I mean, it's dark. The buggy is black. How will they see us?"

"We use battery operated running lights on the back and the front, and we stay over near the shoulder as much as we can. Plus, not all

Amish use them, but in our community, we use battery powered headlights for night driving." He reached down and flipped a switch, and two beams shot out on either side of the front of the buggy. "They don't reach as far as car headlights, but we don't drive as fast, either, so these work fine. There are so many Amish in this area, that most people drive cautiously, but we also do our best to be careful."

"Are there ever accidents?" Maybe she didn't want to know. "Wait!" She held up her hand. "Don't answer that while we're driving, okay? My stomach is jittery enough as it is."

"We're going slow, April. What's making you so nervous?" Jesse reached over and squeezed her fingers and then returned his hand to the reins.

"Was that safe?" She gestured to the reins. "Shouldn't you keep both hands on the reins? I feel so exposed. There are no windows to roll up. No seatbelt. Nothing protecting us."

"I suppose that makes sense." Jesse nodded. "But I'm used to driving with one hand if I need to. The horse is very docile and well trained for driving, so I'm not worried she'll bolt or run away. Plus, we're probably going a whole whopping five miles per hour right now, and we might get up to ten on the road if she's trotting, so it's not like we're racing or anything. I do understand what you mean about feeling exposed, although having been raised riding in buggies, it never bothered me." He clucked to the horse again and turned her onto the paved road.

A few seconds later a car seemed to blast past them. April gasped and reached out for Jesse's arm before realizing she shouldn't grab it while he was driving, per se. She jerked it back. "Sorry."

"It's okay. Scoot over closer and hold onto my arm if you want to." He gave her a reassuring smile. "It's really not that scary. We've only been walking, and at this rate, it's going to be far past bedtime when you arrive, much less when I get home. We're going to pick up the pace a bit."

"No, Jesse! Please." She moved close and slipped her arm through his.

"Aw, come on, sweetheart. It's fine." He smacked his lips, and the horse increased her pace, but at least she wasn't running full out.

"What's she doing? Will she go faster?" The scenery moving by that she could see in the moonlight had definitely increased in speed.

He laughed. "We're only trotting. She could go a lot faster, but we don't gallop on the road unless it's an emergency, so don't worry."

April relaxed her grip on the iron rail and on Jesse's arm but decided she'd stay close to him as she suddenly realized she was starting to enjoy this crazy ride. "I guess this isn't so bad, huh? It might be even nicer in the daytime when I can see everything more clearly."

"It's a date." Jesse gently nudged her with his elbow. "If at all possible, I'll be the one to pick you up in the morning so you can see all the sights on the way back to the house." He pulled back on the reins. "Whoa, Martha."

"What?" April sat up and leaned forward, noticing, for the first time, that they'd stopped in front of a brightly lit house. "We're already here? I thought we'd be driving for a lot longer."

Jesse chuckled. "It's actually only a couple of miles from the farm, since it's a mile or so out of town. It has a charming country setting of its own that you'll see better in the morning. Hold on, and I'll get your bag. Don't worry. I'll set the brake first, and Martha's not going anywhere until I ask her."

"Whew. You read my thoughts."

"I know. I could tell by the look on your

face. Stay there until I come around since you aren't used to climbing out of a buggy at night."

"Or anytime, for that matter."

A few minutes later, Jesse walked her to the front door. "Want me to come in with you?"

"Nah. You'd better get back. It's been a long day, and you need your beauty sleep." She smirked at him when he gave a mock scowl. "I'll take the bag from here. Want a tip for your hard work?"

"Just this." He bent over and placed a soft, lingering kiss on her lips and then sighed. "Good night, Dr. Monroe."

"I'll see you tomorrow. 'Night, Dr. Hardin." She slipped her arms around him and gave him a quick hug. "This was more fun than I expected. Thank you."

He hugged her back then headed for the buggy.

As he stepped in, she waved again. "Sure you're okay on the way home?"

"Yep." He swung the buggy around, showing the shiny reflectors on the back and waved in return. "Sleep well. Tomorrow will be a better day."

Chapter Eight

Where was that girl? It was seven in the morning, and Rachel still wasn't back from gathering the eggs. Esther huffed. She'd have to go look for her again. Why couldn't her daughter be more responsible? This was happening far too often lately, and she wouldn't put up with it much longer. Rumspringa was one thing, but as long as Rachel lived in this house, she needed to keep up with her chores. It wasn't like a house and farm this large would run itself. Thankfully, Levi had already done the milking, but the eggs needed to be cleaned and sorted, the milk separated and put on ice to cool, and the breakfast dishes cleaned.

She stomped out the front door and paused, looking toward the chicken coop and seeing no wayward daughter. More than likely, she was mooning down at the brook again, wasting her time on daydreams. Turning her steps in that direction, she strode along briskly, feeling the ache in her joints this morning even more than usual. She worked to keep an even stride and not limp. She would not allow her age or her joints to keep her from all the tasks that needed completing.

As she drew close to a view of the stream, she slowed her pace and quieted her breathing. Was she being unfair to Rachel? She tried to remember what it had been like at sixteen. She'd had a beau then. Not the man she married, but a boy who'd wanted to court her. Daed hadn't liked him, and it hadn't lasted long. She bit her lip. Jakob was his name. He'd married another girl a couple of years later, and they'd settled down clear across the county and had a family. Why did that memory bring such a pang? She shook her head, trying to ward off the memories. Rachel had many years ahead of her to daydream, but right now, she needed to take care of her chores. She pushed on, rounding the trunk of a large oak. "Rachel? *Vat* are you doing?"

Rachel jumped as though a snake had bit her, and she tried to hide something under her skirt.

"Vat is that you have there?" Esther walked forward and held out her hand. "Give it to me."

When her daughter hesitated, she shook her hand. "Now."

Rachel reluctantly pulled a magazine out from under her skirt.

"Where did you get that?" Esther scowled at what appeared to be a scantily clothed Englisch girl on the cover. "This is no time for going off alone, Rachel. There is too much to do in preparation for the wedding." She took another step forward. "Give it to me."

Rachel handed over the magazine but didn't meet her mother's eyes.

"Did your brudder bring it with him from New York? You tell me the truth, Rachel Hardin. Or did that Englisch woman give it to you?"

"No." Rachel pushed to her feet. "I bought it in town."

"That is worse than if your brudder brought it for you. Why are you so fascinated by the Englisch world? That life will not satisfy you."

Rachel plunked her arms over her chest. "Why are you so against everything in the Englisch world? It seems to have satisfied Jesse. How do you know it won't me as well?"

Esther felt her face grow hot and then cold as she realized what her daughter was implying. "There is no time for this nonsense now. I need you to go to the market. Come to the house for my list, and be sure you bring me the receipt this time." She tucked the magazine under her arm.

"Don't I get my magazine back?"

"Nein. Now go. The list is on the counter by the sink, and the money is in the cookie jar. Don't dawdle at any of the stores either. I need you back soon."

She watched as her youngest fled up the path toward the house. Esther's heart sank. Somehow, she'd lost this child too, and she had no idea what to do about it or how to keep her from leaving. Sorrow over her harsh tone smote her. Was she being too hard on the girl? She didn't want to drive her away, but she couldn't neglect her duty as a mother either. Rachel was already a bit on the wild side, and she must be reined in for her own goot. She shook her head and limped back to the house. Being a parent was not easy, that was for sure.

Jesse watched his little sister holding her skirt up almost to her knees and racing toward the house. What in the world? He followed her at a quick pace and entered the back-kitchen door just seconds after she did. "Rachel?"

She spun around. "What?" A piece of white paper was clutched in her hand. "Oh. It's you. Sorry." Her shoulders sagged, and a tear made its way down her cheek.

He moved forward and enveloped her in a hug. "What's going on?" He drew back and looked into her eyes. "Maam?"

"Ya. I'm sick of it, Jesse. She's always bossing me around. I'm supposed to be on my Rumspringa, but she took my magazine away and told me to get her shopping list and money and go to town. I never have time to myself. How am I supposed to make up my mind about staying or leaving if she keeps this up?"

He dropped his arms from around her. "I hear you, little sister. It's hard. I dealt with Daed more than Maam during my Rumspringa, but it wasn't easy. You do realize they're afraid. I mean, Maam is afraid . . ." His heart lurched as memories of his father and their last argument rushed back. He sucked in a breath and started over. "It's natural for Amish parents to worry their children won't choose to stay in the community . . . in the faith. Maam is scared. You need to try to understand that."

"I suppose." She twisted the string of her capp around her finger. "But it's still not fair."

"I know." He reached out and tweaked her nose like he'd done when she was a small child. "Hey, I'm helping Levi finish fixing the fences. Want to do me a favor and stop by the Bluebird Inn and pick up April?"

His sister's face brightened. "Ya. That would be wunderbar."

He grinned. "Tell her I'm sorry I didn't come, but don't take too much time, or Maam will wonder what's taking you so long with the shopping list."

"*Danke*, Jesse. That sounds goot." She rushed toward the door then spun back and raced to the cookie jar. "I forgot the money." Giggling, she reached in and grabbed the envelope with cash and ran back to the door, slamming the screen behind her.

His mother caught it as it bounced one time. She came in, giving him a long look. "What was all that about? She wasn't that happy when she left me at the stream."

He lifted his chin. "I asked her to pick up April when she finishes her shopping since I'm helping Levi with the fence mending."

"Humph. I'd think that woman would want

to stay at the inn where they have electricity and the modern things she's used to, not come out here with us."

"Maam." Jesse crossed his arms. "I want you to stop treating April like an outsider."

"She is an outsider. She's an Englischer, not Amish." His mother scowled and then turned her back.

"She's my girlfriend, and that makes her family. I'm sorry if that doesn't make you happy, but that's what she is, and you need to choose to accept it."

He heard a soft humph again before he headed to the door, his throat constricting. Now he saw what Rachel was up against, and he wondered if his little sister would end up making the same decision he'd made so many years ago and how much hurt it would continue to cause in their family. Maybe he needed to have a serious talk with his mother once Levi's wedding was behind them. He'd seen the stress heaped on his mother's shoulders with all that needed to be done—it wouldn't be fair to burden her with a confrontation now, but if things didn't change soon, it would have to be done.

April stood at the window of her B&B, basking in the autumn sunshine and taking in the mums and dahlias planted in a bed not far beyond her window. A large shade tree loomed near the front walk, and the paved road was set back far enough from the inn to keep down the road noise. However, she'd been standing here for five minutes and only one car and two buggies had passed in that time, so this was definitely a peaceful spot to stay. The town of Bird-in-Hand was only a short distance down the road, according to Jesse. Maybe she could take a brisk walk to town before he came to pick her up—but first, coffee and a breakfast roll before the little dining room closed.

She hurried down the stairs, coat in hand, taking in all the gorgeous dark wood on the stair railing, the floors, fireplace mantel, and door trim. This place looked to be from another era with the historic furniture, lace curtains, and turn-of-the century charm, but it still offered modern conveniences. She passed an older couple exiting the dining area and slowed. "Any breakfast left?"

A woman she'd seen last night, but barely remembered due to her fatigued brain, walked across the room. A man had checked her in, but she was sure she'd seen this woman as well. Her smile lit up her warm brown-toned skin and dark eyes. She appeared to be in her early thirties, and she radiated peace and confidence, both of which set April at ease. "You bet. Coffee first?" She held up a pot.

"Yes, please." April looked around, wondering if she should help herself or sit.

"You must be April. I'm Tabby. My husband, Bill, checked you in, but I saw you from the office. Also, your sister gave me a heads up what you look like and a bit of your history, so I'd be able to recognize you. Please go ahead and sit. I'm glad you were able to sleep in a bit this morning. You looked beyond tired when you arrived last night. Long day?"

April hung her coat on the back of the chair and eased into a seat at a table covered with a white cloth and set with an exquisite china place setting. "Yes. We drove here from New York and then spent time with Jesse Hardin's family." Warmth flooded her cheeks. "He's my boyfriend."

"Ah, I see. An Englischer and an Amish man. That must have made for an interesting supper." She poured coffee into April's mug.

"Well, yes. Although Jesse left home after

his Rumspringa, and he didn't remain in the Amish faith. So I guess he's an Englischer now too."

Tabby nodded. "Did you sleep all right? Everything okay with your room?"

"It's perfect. I loved watching the birds in the birdbath and the kittens scampering across the lawn. Plus, your flowers look amazing. I slept like a rock. In fact, so well it would be nice to just stay in that room the entire trip." She bit her lip, wondering if she'd said too much.

"The whole area is that way—peaceful, quiet, and lots of comfortable Amish furniture."

Tabby headed for the kitchen. "Pancakes and eggs with a side of fresh fruit sound all right for breakfast? A side of orange juice or apple?"

"Sounds wonderful, thank you. OJ would be great."

A few minutes later as April poured what appeared to be homemade blueberry syrup across her pancakes, Tabby refilled her coffee and then sank into a chair across the table. "I don't mean to pry, and you can tell me to mind my own business if you'd like to, but I'm wondering—how has your visit been with the Hardins so far?"

April gave her a brief summary of the

conversation about conventional, modern medicine but tried her best to not make Jesse's mom sound like a shrew. She swirled her last bite of pancake in the syrup and savored the taste. "So, not the best start to my visit, but I'm hoping it gets better."

Tabby sighed. "I'm sorry to hear that. Many of the Amish are very stubborn about modern medicine. Actually, modern anything. I wish there were more doctors around here to choose from."

"Thanks. Too bad Jesse's mom feels that way, but it is what it is. I can't change her, but hopefully, she'll soften as she gets to know me. She didn't ask Jesse anything about his veterinarian practice, so I'm guessing she's not overly fond of his occupation, either."

Tabby took a drink of her coffee, set down the cup, and met April's gaze. "At least Jesse is in your corner. That's worth a lot. He sounds like a good guy."

"He is. Which is why I'm hoping his mom will eventually like me. I hit it off with his brother Levi and sister Rachel, but Esther—Mrs. Hardin—has a huge wall built around her where Englischers are concerned."

"I get that. I've lived here for years now.

Most Amish are very good, hardworking people, but they don't trust outsiders easily. It took Bill and me several years before many of them would do more than nod when they passed us in the market, but now we have several Amish friends. Hang in there. It will get better."

The *clip-clop* of a horse's hooves sounded through the window, and April peered beyond the gauzy white curtains. "That must be Jesse. Thank you for everything, Tabby. The breakfast and the encouraging talk."

Tabby came around the table and gave April a quick hug. "You've got this, girl. Don't give up. It will work out. In fact, if you're a praying girl, you might ask for a bit of divine assistance. That's what He's all about, you know. He loves you and the Amish equally. Remember that when you're dealing with Mrs. H."

April smiled. "Good reminder. I tend to forget that too often. Thanks, Tabby." She grabbed her jacket from the back of the chair. Thankfully, she always kept her phone in her pocket and had a bit of cash and a credit card in the phone case as well since she wasn't big on lugging a purse around all day. She hurried outside, slipping her arms into the jacket as she pushed out the door. She stopped short. Jesse wasn't in the buggy. Rachel sat in the seat, confidently holding the reins. "Oh, hi, Rachel. I thought Jesse was coming to get me?"

"Goot morning, April. Jesse's helping some of the men set up for the wedding, so he asked me to get you. He said he also needed to finish a fence post he'd promised to get done for Levi, so he has his hands full of work today. I was going to pick up Maam's groceries before I came here, but then I decided you might enjoy stopping at the store. Is that all right?"

"Sure. I don't mind at all." April climbed up and sat next to Rachel, feeling a bit more confident now that it was daylight and she could see where they were going. "Is it far to the store?"

"Only about a mile, if that. Martha will make it in no time." Rachel scooted over to give April a bit more room.

"Um—no offense—but are you old enough to drive this thing? I mean, are there laws on how old you have to be to drive a buggy on the road?"

Rachel shook her head. "You don't need a license for a horse and buggy, and I've been driving since I was fourteen. Levi taught me when I was twelve, but they didn't allow me to drive alone for a couple of years." She flicked the reins and clucked to the horse, and the buggy jerked forward, making April rock against the back of the seat.

April grabbed the wrought-iron railing next to her, wondering if this was such a great idea. However, the ride smoothed out, and they'd only exchanged a few words when Rachel expertly brought the horse to a stop at a long hitching rail in front of a small market that also housed a café, from the sign hanging over the door. The building was made of rustic logs, but several large flower pots lined the porch, each boasting different colors of geraniums still in bloom. The windows sparkled as though recently cleaned, and soothing music emanated from the open door.

Rachel jumped down from the buggy and went forward to tie up her horse. She waved at April. "Come on. You're welcome to shop with me if you want to." She waved at an Amish girl exiting the store and an Amish boy carrying an iPhone.

April took a closer look at the girl. Was that faint lipstick she saw on her mouth? These two looked to be about Rachel's age, and she guessed they might be in their Rumspringa as well. She'd bet their parents weren't too pleased about the makeup and modern technology their children were using, but from what she understood, that's what this time period was for—to figure out if they wanted to stay or leave their community.

She caught up with Rachel and stepped into the store, loving the cozy ambiance it gave off. Rustic, but soothing and friendly somehow.

Rachel grabbed a basket and then pulled out her list. She began moving along the aisles at a fast pace, placing items into her basket. The last one was a large bag of cheese, and after laying it in the basket, she reached out and grabbed a second one.

"Wow. That's a lot of cheese. What do you plan to make?"

"Levi asked for macaroni and cheese and a big salad on the side. Maam is baking bread, so I don't have to worry about that, but she wants fresh produce too." Rachel headed for the produce section with April walking beside her.

"Tell me about Englischer weddings." Rachel said as she reached for a large head of red-tipped lettuce.

"What exactly would you like to know?"

"Everything. I've only seen an Amish wedding, but I heard that the brides wear beautiful white gowns."

"Yes, that's typical. The groom often wears a tuxedo, unless it's a country wedding and they choose a different type of venue and clothing. The ceremony usually has music, prayers, vows, and often there's a reception afterwards—sometimes with music and dancing. It's really kind of up to the bride and groom what they want to plan. There's always a big cake, and sometimes they feed each other a bite after they cut it together. The bride throws her bouquet to the single women after the reception, and tradition says, the one who catches it will be the next one to marry."

Rachel raised her brows. "You mean their parents don't decide for them? Sounds amazing."

April laughed. "I'll bet Amish weddings are fun and beautiful as well."

Rachel looked off into the distance, a dreamy expression on her face. "The bride doesn't wear a white gown. Just her best dress. No music. I wish there was music. And dancing. That would be wunderbar."

April's heart melted for this girl who

teetered on the edge of womanhood but still sounded like a wistful child at times. How hard to be pulled two different directions and have to make a decision for your life at such a young age. "Jesse told me that the Amish don't really use musical instruments or play much music."

Rachel stopped at the bin of cucumbers and grabbed a few. "Ya. The church lets us bend the rules during Rumspringa. Me and my friends listen to the radio all the time. I really like Beyoncé."

"Really?" April tried not to act too surprised, but she doubted Mrs. Hardin would approve of that choice. "It's nice you're able to have choices right now."

"She just seems so happy and full of life when she sings . . . and free . . ."

"I get that, Rachel, but no one in my world feels that way all the time. We have to make hard choices too. We go to work, pay bills, live with loss and hurt and disappointments. It can be busy, crowded, noisy. A big city can be downright scary at times as well. It's not like your community here, where everyone knows everyone else, and most of them are friendly. You can walk down a street in New York and rarely even make eye contact with anyone, much less have a person ever speak to you. Why, I've even been in fast food places and little markets where even the vendors were grumpy. It can be very hard to find your place in a city or to make friends."

Rachel just stared at her without replying, and April took the hint. "Hey, sorry." April held up her hands. "You don't have to listen to me or your mom or anyone else. It's your decision what you do with your life. I just want you to know that being an Englischer doesn't mean you'll have a glamorous life."

"Thanks, April." This time a smile peeked out. "I appreciate it." She bit her lip. "Last night . . . what Maam said about doctors. I hope you know she doesn't speak for all of us."

"That means a lot, Rachel." She reached out and gave the girl a quick hug.

Rachel walked toward the checkout counter. "Ever try Amish rock candy? Come on. I'll buy you a piece before we head home."

Chapter Nine

Jesse helped Levi and two other Amish men from their community set up tables and chairs outside for the reception and dinner at their home that would follow the wedding at Sarah's father's home while a couple of teen boys erected a volleyball net. Thankfully, the two farms were close neighbors, so it was an easy drive from the wedding to the reception, since all Amish weddings took place at the bride's family home. Jesse kept looking toward the road, wondering what was taking his sister and April so long. Hopefully, April didn't get scared riding in the buggy again. He grinned. He'd enjoyed teasing her a bit last night as well as showing her a side of his life she'd never experienced before.

Steps sounded behind him, and he turned expectantly, wondering if he'd somehow missed the buggy's arrival. Naomi Trotter walked toward him, a smile gracing her lovely face. "Your mother is looking for you, Levi. You and

Sarah need to go over the seating for the head table with her."

Levi rolled his eyes. "I thought we'd decided that. We've been over it more than once already. Is she in the kitchen?"

"Ya, where else? Waiting for you."

Levi started to set the chair down that he'd been about to take to the table, but Naomi held out her hands. "I'll take that for you and stay and help Jesse." They spent a few minutes setting chairs in place in comfortable silence. Naomi peeked up at Jesse when she set a chair down next to the one he'd placed. "It's been a long time since we attended a wedding together. Eli and Emily Yoder's if I remember correctly."

"I'm sure you do." Jesse didn't like the way this conversation was headed, although he'd always thought Naomi was a nice enough girl, but he'd never been serious about her in the way he knew she'd hoped.

"You don't?" She stopped and looked at him, her eyes wide. "No distant but good memories coming back?" She gave him a smile that again made him want to take a step away.

He shrugged. "Maybe a few."

Naomi took a step closer. "I know you have a life in New York, but you know you'll always be welcome here if you ever decide . . ." Her voice trailed into silence as she continued to stare at Jesse.

A horse's hooves broke the now uncomfortable silence, and Jesse took another step back. They turned to see a buggy pulling into the yard holding a laughing Rachel and April. Jesse gave Naomi a curt nod. "Excuse me." He jogged over to meet the girls. "Rachel, I'll tie up Martha. Maam is waiting for the groceries in the kitchen." He grinned at the laughing girls. "I hope you didn't run this horse."

April tossed her head. "Ha. Don't be a hypocrite. I could name another Hardin who enjoys speed." She met his gaze and giggled again. "Seriously, it was a lot of fun this time." She waited until he tied the horse. Then she accepted the hand he offered to help her down and jumped to the ground.

"Find everything you needed?"

She nodded. "Rachel did. She had the list. I was only along for the ride."

"April bought nearly a pound of rock candy after I gave her one to try. She loved it." Rachel spoke over her shoulder as she took the bag of groceries from the buggy.

"I'm not going to eat it all myself. I bought it to share."

Jesse moved over beside Rachel. "Can you handle the groceries? I'd like to borrow April for a sec." He slipped his arm around April's waist and drew her close, as much to show April how much he cared as Naomi.

"Ya, go ahead. See you later, April." She hoisted the bag into her arms and headed for the house.

Jesse gave April a squeeze. "See? I told you my family would fall in love with you."

"We had a lot of fun together. Rachel reminds me a little of you."

"Oh, really! Well, don't tell Maam that." He gave her another light squeeze and then dropped his arm. "I took you for a complete city girl, April Monroe, but small-town life looks very good on you."

"Yeah?" She tipped her head to the side and winked. "Maybe I could keep it up for a while. It's pretty nice here."

Jesse held her gaze for several heartbeats, and it was all he could do not to drop his head and kiss her. Somehow, he didn't think that would go over well in his conservative Amish community with so many neighbors milling around. He took her hand instead and tugged her toward the tables. "Come on. I'll show you what we've been doing."

Two Amish women were placing decorative centerpieces of flowers and candles on one of the nearby tables. April had assumed everything would be very plain, but this was lovely. "So this is what an Amish reception looks like. I love it. The simplicity is perfect but still very pretty."

Jesse poked her in the side. "You ever think about this stuff? You know, getting married some day?"

April glanced at him to see if he was serious, but his face wore a broad smile. "'Pft. No. I'm way too busy."

"Huh. I thought all women fantasized about their wedding day."

She matched his grin and added a giggle. "Fine. Sure. I want a huge, romantic wedding. Long white gown with a train, a band playing soft music, a hunky groom in a tux, and tons of Amish rock candy." She snorted. "There. You happy now?"

"Rock candy, huh? Good to know." Then his expression turned serious.

She slapped him on the arm, then she stilled. "Why? Do you ever think about it?" This was the first time they'd really talked about this subject, and her heart was pounding.

He gave her a look she couldn't quite decipher when movement from the doorway caught her attention, and she pivoted.

Rachel waved at them. "I have a surprise for you!"

"A surprise?" She looked at Jesse. "What should I do?"

"Go." Jesse nodded toward the house. "I still have more work helping to set up. Go see what Rachel's up to, and I'll be in when I can." He gave her a reassuring pat on her arm and then turned back to the men still setting up chairs.

April hated to leave him after the fun banter they'd had about marriage—but had it only been teasing, or had she seen something deeper in Jesse's eyes? Was all this wedding preparation affecting him to the degree he might be thinking of proposing? If he did, what would she say? They'd only been dating for six months, and she'd always assumed she'd remain single and dedicated to her career for several more years. She headed to the house, deciding to shelve the thoughts unless Jesse did something else to rekindle them.

Rachel nearly pulled her in the door when she opened it. "Hurry. I have something to show you." She put her finger to her lips and beckoned April to follow, her movements stealthy and quiet.

April walked behind Rachel into a bedroom on the second floor, up the stairs from the living area and farthest from the kitchen. "Is this your room?" She looked around, noting the starkness of the furnishings and the use of very little color. Somehow, she couldn't see the vivacious teen living in this room.

"No. It's Maam's." Rachel pointed at a dress laying on the bed. "See? I found a dress for you to wear." She scooped it up and held the deep purple fabric by the shoulders and twirled around. "I thought if you wore it, you could fit in better tomorrow at the reception."

The dress didn't appear to be new, but it was in excellent condition, with sleeves that would come halfway between her elbow and her wrist, a fitted waist and calf-length, narrow skirt. "It's lovely, but are you sure it's all right?"

Somehow, she couldn't see Mrs. Hardin sending Rachel up to show her this dress. That would be the last thing she'd expect to have happen.

"Sure. Maam doesn't wear it anymore, and I think it would fit you perfectly. Don't you want to try it on?" She shoved it into April's hands.

April held it up in front of herself. "Do you have a mirror?"

"Nein. The Amish don't use mirrors." She made a face. "It could lead to vanity."

"Oh. I see."

"Naomi Trotter will be shaking in her prayer capp." Rachel giggled as she watched April look down at the dress.

Steps clomped into the room, and both girls whirled around.

Esther stood inside the door, her lips pressed into a straight line. "What are you doing in my room?" She reached out and yanked the dress out of April's hands. "Why do you have my dress?"

"Maam! I told April she could wear it tomorrow."

"She absolutely cannot wear it. Nein. She does not have my permission."

"You never wear it anymore. You haven't worn it since Daed died."

Mrs. Hardin winced and looked away. Then she turned a fierce expression on Rachel. "That does not mean you can loan it out to just anyone. Now get to the kitchen and help the ladies prepare the rest of the food for tomorrow." She pointed out the door.

"Yes, Maam." Rachel shot a look at April. "Sorry, April."

"Sorry to April?" Mrs. Hardin huffed. "You should be apologizing to your mother." Esther didn't so much as glance at April but left her standing in the middle of the room as she tromped downstairs.

Now what? Right now, going back to the B&B and taking a nap sounded like a great plan, but she needed to face this and apologize. She probably wouldn't want a stranger barging into her room and acting like she was going to try on her clothes either. Yes, she definitely must apologize.

As she entered the kitchen it appeared Mrs. Hardin hadn't finished chastising her daughter. "That dress was not yours to give. You need to learn to think before you act, daughter."

The two other Amish women sitting at the table preparing vegetables kept their heads bent over their work, seemingly not wanting to intrude on the public family altercation. April stood in the doorway, wondering if she should retreat or continue forward.

Rachel swung from the sink and glared at her mother. "I like her. I was trying to help."

"Ya. You like anything Englisch, and that's the problem with you, I think." Mrs. Hardin planted her hands on her hips and returned the glare. "Mark my words, if you continue down this road, it will lead you to trouble. Your place is here. Just like your brudder."

Rachel narrowed her eyes, but April thought she saw a glint of tears shining in them before she turned away. "That's for me to decide, ya?"

April moved into the room a step. "I'm so sorry, Mrs. Hardin. I didn't mean to offend you. Rachel only wanted to help me blend in tomorrow. I wasn't trying to cause trouble in your family."

"You have already done that. You are Englisch. We are Amish. You will never blend in."

She draped the dress over the back of a chair in the corner, her face flushed beyond what it should have been.

It was warm, but April didn't like the way

she was breathing either. Short and a bit choppy. Could it only be from emotional exertion or was it something else? "Are you feeling all right, Mrs. Hardin?"

"I am quite well, danke." However, her breaths turned to something close to gasps.

April frowned and strode forward. "Please. Sit down. We'll get you a glass of water. You don't sound well at all."

The older woman glared, but her hand fumbled for the back of a chair, and she pulled it toward her and sank into it. Her cheeks had gone from flushed to pale in a matter of seconds.

Rachel hurried to pour water into a glass and handed it to her mother.

April waited for her to drink it. "Better?"

"Ya. I think so."

"Have you had many episodes like this where you've had difficulty breathing? Been lightheaded or faint?"

"Ya. A few. But it's nothing, I'm sure."

"When do they usually happen?"

"Around mealtime, I suppose."

April took a step closer, wishing she could take the woman's pulse and aching for her medical bag. She'd bring it with her the next time she came here from the B&B. "Did all of this begin around the same time you started getting sore joints?"

Esther started to rise. "I need to get back to work." She winced as she tried to stand and then sat back down. "I'll be fine in a moment. I've just been on my feet a lot the last few days with this wedding and all."

April wanted to pat the woman's shoulder, but she doubted it would be well-received. "I'm guessing you won't want to hear this, Mrs. Hardin, but this may be adult-onset diabetes. I would strongly suggest you get testing done before it progresses further."

"I'm fine." She waved her hand as though at a pesky fly.

"Diabetes can be very serious if not treated. You could start by adjusting your diet. I could make a few suggestions if you'd like to hear them."

Esther planted the palms of her hands on the table and pushed to her feet. "I do not think I can say it more plainly that I am not interested in your medical opinions, nor anyone else's. Please do not talk to me about this again." She stood shakily and then tipped her head as though forced to speak her next words. "Thank you for the glass of water and for asking about me."

"You're welcome. I'll go see if Jesse needs any help." April knew when it was time to leave, and now was that time. She spun around and headed for the door.

"April?"

She turned slowly at the change of tone she heard in Mrs. Hardin's voice. It had softened somehow. "Yes?"

"You may wear my dress tomorrow. Rachel was right. I have no use for it, and if it would make you feel more comfortable, I won't begrudge you that."

"Thank you, ma'am. I appreciate that very much."

Esther plucked the dress off the back of the chair and handed to April, who took it hesitantly, and then clutched it against her chest and fled from the room.

Esther watched the young Englischer leave the kitchen, hugging the dress to her chest. So many conflicting emotions spun through her thoughts and heart right now. Longing for her dear husband to be here tomorrow for the first wedding in their family. Fear at the idea she could lose her only daughter. Shame at the way she had treated this young woman who had only tried to help. She'd seen the little glance of wonder Rachel had given her when she'd offered the dress to April. Did her daughter really think she had no heart or kindness anywhere in her body for strangers? Was that how she appeared to others?

She glanced at the two women still busily paring vegetables and pretending nothing had happened. The Amish way. Do not interfere into another's business unless asked. Well, it was a good way. Of course, the bishop would be called if a person were to cross a line that required a reprimand, but most of their people wouldn't speak their piece in another's home.

Rachel brushed by her and lightly touched her shoulder. She looked up at her daughter's sweet face. "Danke, Maam. For the dress." She gave a fleeting smile and moved back to her work at the sink.

Warmth spread through Esther's heart. That was the first time in months Rachel had touched her. How long had it been since she'd tried to hug Rachel? Too long, for sure and for certain. Children needed touch and reassurance even if they were in their Rumspringa. She'd try to remember that after this. Maybe not get so angry at her little girl when she made decisions that didn't suit the Amish way. Was that what she'd done to Jesse? Driven him off when he'd been trying to decide what was best for his life? She placed her hand over her chest, a sharp pain stabbing inside, but this time she knew it wasn't from a physical ailment, but from the pain of a mother's heart.

Chapter Ten

JESSE AND LEVI STOOD AT THE barn's open double doors at Sarah's parents' home, letting the fresh air filter through into the open space beyond. A few tables covered with white linen were placed around the space in the center where hay bales had once been stacked. It was far different from what Jesse had seen at weddings in New York, but he knew Sarah would be pleased with the flowers and candles on the tables and the white cloths draping the doors. He turned and slung his arm around Levi's shoulders. "It's hard to believe my little brother will be married this time tomorrow. Where has time gone these past few years?"

"I'm glad you're here, Jesse. I was worried you might not come now that you're settled in your Englisch life so far away. Plus, you have your business to look after, and you have a busy life. Thank you for making the time for me and Sarah." He glanced over his shoulder. "For Maam and Rachel as well, even though I know things haven't been easy with Maam."

"I'll never be too busy for family, Levi. It's been harder for April, I think, but she's trying hard to win Maam over."

Levi straightened from leaning against the barn door. "Not an easy challenge, for sure and for certain. I'm sorry she hasn't felt welcome." He slapped Jesse on the back. "I imagine wedding bells aren't too far in your future, ya?"

"I don't know . . . I mean, I have thought about it, but I guess we'll have to see."

"Be honest, brudder, you have strong feelings for her. I see it every time you look at her. I'm a man in love, and I can recognize it in others when I see it. What are your intentions toward her? They are honest, ya?"

Jesse tried to keep a sober face while he reached into his trouser pocket. "You aren't to tell anyone." He withdrew a small box and held it out. "I've been carrying this around since before we left New York, waiting for the right time. It might be this weekend if that's all right with you? I don't want to steal your special day if you'd rather I wait."

Levi opened the box, and Jesse moved close to see the sparkling solitaire diamond set in white gold. "Of course, it's all right with me.

April seems like a very good woman. Sweet, kind, and understanding. The kind of woman you'd want as a mother to your children. You have my approval, and Rachel's too, I'm sure."

"I appreciate that." He tucked the box back where it came from, and they headed to the house.

Levi matched his pace to Jesse's. "I'll admit it's a little bittersweet. . . both of us starting new lives but living so far apart. I always dreamed of our children growing up together, running the farm, and playing with the animals and such. It's going to be hard when you marry and start a family while living in New York."

Jesse nodded, trying to force words past the tightness in his throat. "I didn't realize how much I've missed this community . . . and all of you. I'm sorry I haven't come to visit more often, but I plan to change that."

Levi bumped his shoulder with Jesse's. "It's all right, brudder. We have always walked different paths—me with my love for farming, you with a desire to care for animals. I don't expect you to change your life because I miss you."

Jesse was hit again with a homesickness he'd never expected. It had been easy to leave when he was eighteen and excited about starting a new adventure, but he had a feeling it was going to be much harder this time.

A few hours later, April finished drying the supper dishes and hung the dishtowel she'd been using over a hook on the wall. She smiled at Rachel. "I think that takes care of the last of the pots and pans." She placed a hand at the small of her back and stretched. "I can see why your mother has aches and pains being on her feet for so long. I thought walking the halls of a hospital and waiting on patients was hard work, but it's nothing to the constant care of a home and family, on top of putting on a wedding. I don't know how she's kept up with it all."

Rachel plunked down on a chair. "Ach, I know. I'm way younger than you, and my feet hurt too."

April raised her brows. "Way younger? You make me sound as though I'm ancient."

Rachel giggled. "Well, twelve years feels like a lot to me. But I guess you aren't ancient. Yet."

"Hey!" April lightly punched the girl on the shoulder and chuckled. "Thanks for that. I think."

Jesse walked in and beckoned to April. "You ready to go? I got the tire fixed and put on the car, so I can get you back quickly tonight." He glanced out the window. "It's just getting dark, so I thought you'd prefer that to the buggy this time."

"That's great you got it fixed, but I think I'd like to take the buggy again if it's not too much work for you? I mean, I know you're tired and you'd have to harness the horse, so if it's too much . . . ?"

"Not at all, but I thought it made you nervous?" Jesse took a step closer and pulled her to his side.

"It does, but it helped riding with Rachel. Besides, I've always believed it's important to conquer your fears, so this ride tonight should help."

Jesse gave a slow nod and a tiny smile tipped his lips. "Good point. All right, we'll do it. You wait here, and I'll bring the buggy around."

Fifteen minutes later, Jesse walked April out to the buggy. She headed toward the passenger side, and he stopped her. "No. I have an idea I'd like you to consider." He led her toward the driver's side. "I want you to drive tonight."

She took a step back. "No. No way. I can't do that. I'd wreck us." April backed up another step.

"You won't. I promise. I'll sit close and help you. I can even keep my hands on the reins with yours until you're comfortable. You said you wanted to conquer your fears, right?"

She nodded, not sure this was exactly what she'd had in mind. "Yes, but . . ."

"This is the best way to do it. You'll see there's nothing to fear when you're holding the reins and guiding the horse."

"But she doesn't know me. I won't know what to do, and Martha will know that." She tried to keep the quiver out of her voice but didn't quite make it.

"Come on, April. If it's too scary after the first few minutes, we'll trade places." He put his hand over hers and squeezed.

"You must try it, April."

April swung around, not sure she'd heard correctly. "Mrs. Hardin?"

"It is not goot to let fear rule your life." She gave a slow, somber nod. "This I know in my heart. You should drive the horse tonight."

April blinked back the tears that had sprung to her eyes." Shock had almost rooted her to the spot at the woman's words. She couldn't believe Mrs. Hardin had spoken kindly and given her advice. There was no way she could ignore that gesture. "All right." The words came out in a whisper, and she tried again. "All right. I will. Thank you, Mrs. Hardin."

Mrs. Hardin nodded but said nothing more, just watched as April walked around the buggy to the driver's side.

April climbed into the buggy and settled in the seat Jesse usually took, waiting for him to come around and climb in beside her.

He scooted close and picked up the reins. "Put your hands here, and grip them firmly, but not too tight."

He waited while she complied. "Firm and steady, so you can feel the horse through the reins. If she pulls at the reins, you're putting too much pressure on her mouth, and you can give a little. That's why I said not too tight. If it's too loose, she'll get lazy and decide to stop and graze." He grinned. "No worries this one will run away. She likes her feed too much for that."

The tension in April's shoulders eased a little at his words. "Okay. Light, firm, and steady." She grasped the reins and looked at him. "Now what?"

"Cluck to her and shake the reins a little so she feels them on her back."

"Whew. Okay." She turned and waved at Mrs. Hardin. "Thank you again for your encouragement." Something like a brief frown flickered across the woman's face but then disappeared. She gave a quick nod and disappeared into the house. April huffed out a small breath. "Here goes." She made a clucking sound and lightly shook the reins, and Martha moved forward at a slow, sedate pace. "She's moving!" April wasn't sure whether to drop the reins and panic or beam with pride.

Jesse laughed. "Which is what you asked her to do."

"Now what?" April gripped the reins tight and then realized what she was doing. "Light, firm, and steady. Light, firm, and steady. I can do this." She kept her attention straight forward between the horse's ears at the place on the road where the beams of the two headlights hit, thankful they were moving at such a slow pace.

"You are doing it. Perfectly, if I may say so." Jesse placed his hands on his knees and leaned against the back of the seat.

"Don't move away, Jesse. I might need you." April bit her lip and concentrated. "What do I do when we get to the end of the driveway?"

"You tug on the rein to the right, and she'll turn right. She knows the way to town, so it's not going to take much. We rarely go to the left unless we're visiting a neighbor."

"Okay. Tug to the right. Light, firm, and steady." April knit her brows together, hoping she could remember it all. A few minutes later, the drive ended at the road, and she sucked in a breath. "Now?"

"Now. A light tug on the right rein."

She followed Jesse's instructions, and Martha obediently turned to the right and clip-clopped out onto the paved road. "What if a car comes?"

"We'll see its headlights way before it comes, and I'll help you keep her over on the edge of the road. Remember, we have bright reflectors on the back, so they'll see us as they approach and go around us. It'll be fine."

A grin split April's lips. "I'm doing this. I'm really doing this. She's walking straight down the road and not trying to run away. It's not that scary at all."

Jesse sat next to April on the covered porch of the Sunflower Inn after tying Martha to the railing and helping April down. "You did fantastic driving a buggy for your first time." Pride welled in his chest that this amazing woman had conquered her fear and gone a step beyond what she'd thought she could do. After only two rides in a buggy, she'd taken the reins in her hands and kept control.

April sighed. "That was actually a lot of fun. I'm going to want to do it again, you know?" She arched a brow at him. "You may have to relegate yourself to being a backseat driver from now on."

"Ha!" He gave a shout of laughter. "You think so, huh? One drive and I'm off the driver's seat forever? How do you like that?" He pointed up at the twinkling stars peppering the vivid deep blue sky. "It's so clear here. So fresh and clean."

She looked up. "You can't even see one star when you're in New York City. It's either the tall buildings in the way or smog or you just never think to stop and look up. It's almost as pretty up there as it is down here." She waved a hand in front of them at their surroundings.

He draped an arm around her, and she

snuggled close. "I guess I never realized how much I'd lost—how much I'd miss this—when I left."

April arched her brows and looked at him. "I'm sorry to hear that."

"No. It's all right." He gave her a squeeze. "I gained a lot as well." He meant that, from the bottom of his heart, and he prayed she could hear it in his voice. Was this the right time? The time he'd been waiting for? It surely couldn't be a more romantic setting.

"I wouldn't mind settling down in a small town like this someday."

He leaned forward and looked at her, his heartbeat quickening. "Really? How about New York? The hospital? Your plans to move up and gain a permanent position there?"

"I'm just fantasizing here. Run with it a minute. I mean, in a small town, I could open my own practice without so many patients getting shoved through where I'm told I can only take fifteen minutes for each one or get yelled at for spending too much time with a patient I feel needs the extra care. I could be my own boss. If you had a vet clinic nearby, we could meet for lunch every day. I could go home to a small house every night with fresh air, a little garden, and maybe a cat or a dog." She sighed.

"That sounds about perfect." He leaned in and gave her a soft kiss, wondering if she could hear his heart racing.

April put her head on his shoulder. "This has been so nice. I had no idea I'd love it here when you invited me to come. Thank you for bringing me. I didn't know this side of you existed, but I love it."

Now. It had to be now. "April, there's something I've been wanting to ask you."

April shot upright and pulled away from him right as his hand went to his pocket. "Look! A shooting star. I've never seen one before. Did you see it, Jesse?" She jumped to her feet and took a step toward the edge of the porch.

Jesse chuckled. "That was an airplane or a jet, I'm guessing, from the speed it was moving."

"Oh." Her shoulders slumped. "I guess that would have been my next guess." She covered a yawn with her hand. "I'm sorry. I didn't realize I was so tired. My eyes must be playing tricks on me. Like your mother said, it's going to be a busy day tomorrow, and we need to get some sleep." She held out her hand to him.

He took it and allowed her to pull him to his feet. The moment had passed. He'd missed it.

Somehow, he'd have to hope another one came along as perfect at this.

"What's the schedule tomorrow?" She slipped her hand through the crook of his arm.

"There's a short ceremony for the Amish family and close friends, then any Englisch guests join us for the reception. Levi got the bishop's permission for me to attend the wedding even though I'm no longer Amish."

"That's good. I'm so glad you can be there for your brother." She squeezed his arm. "Oh. What were you saying before the plane came and I interrupted? You said you wanted to ask me something."

"It can wait. I'm a bit tired too, and I'd best get home." He leaned down and gave her another soft kiss. "Good night. Sleep well, and I'll pick you up in the morning."

Chapter Eleven

THE ROOSTER HAD CROWED LESS THAN two hours ago, and daylight broke not far after, but Jesse and Levi stood in Levi's room getting ready for the big day. Jesse held Levi's coat while he slipped his arms into the sleeves then turned and tugged at the base of his jacket and fiddled with his black bow tie, only worn for weddings. "How do I look?" Levi faced Jesse, his expression intense.

"Like a man about to get married. Quite handsome and almost settled. Very respectable." Jesse inspected the brand-new black suit his brother wore and then picked up the flat-brimmed hat and tamped it down on Levi's head. "Very Amish."

Levi gave him a playful shove. "Smart-aleck."

"Seriously, you look great. Sarah is a lucky woman."

"Nein." Levi shook his head. "It is I who am blessed."

Jesse picked up a black jacket from the bed and slipped his arms into it, then placed a hat on his head and turned for Levi's inspection.

"I'm surprised you kept your suit all these years."

"I took it with me. It was one thing I couldn't leave behind. Not sure why. I'm surprised it still fits." He ran his hand down the front of the jacket. "We'd better get over to Sarah's parents' farm. Sarah is probably waiting, and it's time to get you to the ceremony."

Levi drew in a long breath. "Ya. It is. Let's go." He headed toward the door like a man anxious to meet his destiny.

Jesse nodded. "Are we driving Maam and Rachel over?"

"Nein. Maam wants to stay here a few minutes longer to make sure all the food is ready. We'll take the surrey, and Rachel will drive Maam in the enclosed buggy. We'd better hurry, though. I don't want Sarah to worry that I'll be late."

A few minutes later, they pulled to a stop at the neighboring farm, and Jesse and Levi spotted Sarah and her father at the same time. Sarah wore a sky-blue dress, a matching cape, and a black prayer capp rather than the typical, daily white one. It startled Jesse for a moment. Then he remembered that was tradition for a bride.

Levi stepped forward and offered his arm. "You look lovely."

Soft color rose to her cheeks. "Danke. You look very nice too." She took his arm and they walked toward the barn together, her two younger sisters serving as attendants following.

Jesse stood outside, hoping his mother and Rachel arrived soon. He pushed back the sleeve of his black jacket and peeked at his watch. The ceremony would start in fifteen minutes. The bishop was nothing, if not punctual. The creek of wheels made him pivot. Another thing that needed to be done before he left—the axles on the buggy needed greasing. He couldn't really fault his little brother for not getting it all done, what with courting Sarah, the care of the farm after Daed's passing, and the things needing done in the short time after the wedding announcement had been made.

Jesse walked to the buggy and offered a hand to his mother. "Maam, I'm glad you made it early."

His mother took it and stepped carefully down the step to the ground. "Rachel, tie up the horse. Then come along and join us, you hear? No dawdling with your friends." She placed her hand above her eyes against the glare of the sun and then motioned to someone nearby.

Naomi stood not ten feet away, her expression expectant and hopeful.

Maam reached out a hand. "You will sit with us, Naomi. You are practically family, ya?" She looked from Jesse to Naomi, and Jesse's stomach turned sour. He'd thought Maam had accepted April was his girlfriend, but here she went again, trying to push Naomi at him.

Naomi moved toward Jesse and took his other arm. "I'd love to. Danke." She gave him a smile that contained more than a little flirtatiousness. "It's just as I remember the last time we attended a wedding together. Almost like no time has passed."

Jesse squirmed at the words, wishing April were here at his side and allowed to take part in the ceremony. "I don't know about that. It's kind of a faint memory for me."

She gave him a radiant smile. "You tease me. I'm sure you remember our time together quite well." She sobered and stepped a little closer. "You coming here for Levi's wedding means a great deal to him. To all of us, actually."

"I'm grateful the bishop allowed me to attend the ceremony."

"I never doubted he would." She gave him an appraising look as they walked toward the barn. "Anyone can see by looking at you that you're still one of us. Well . . ." She huffed a soft laugh. "Anyone who is present, that is, and who belongs." She raised a brow and leaned across him toward his mother. "Will Dr. Monroe be attending today?"

Jesse cut in before his mother could reply, although he saw her lips part and guessed she was going to say she hoped not. "Yes. She'll be here for the reception." He pulled away from Naomi's tight hold on his arm and bowed toward the open doorway. "We're here. After you." He'd sit as far from her as he could if he had any say about it.

Naomi smiled, stopped, and then put an arm across her middle and winced. Then she straightened.

What was that about? Right now, he didn't really care. He'd guess it was Naomi hoping to get sympathy and attention for some pretend ailment, but he wasn't going to fall for that. He hurried inside, leaving his mother and Naomi to follow, but he couldn't miss his mother's voice talking to Naomi's father as he drew near. "Hello, Daniel. Poor Jesse. That Englisch girl has my son all mixed up."

Esther took the arm Daniel Trotter offered and followed him slowly toward the barn, thankful the wedding was always held at the bride's home. All of the food preparation had been enough, without having to be in charge of this part as well. The boys had done a fine job getting it all set up with the help of the Amish community, of course. She turned her thoughts back to the man walking beside her and lowered her voice a little. No need for anyone to start saying she was a gossip. "There must be something we can do to help Naomi and Jesse get back together. We always thought our two children would be wed one day, ya?"

"That we did, Esther. But they are adults, and it is not our place. As much as I'd like to see them wed, we must not interfere." He squeezed her hand against his side as though to soften the words.

"I suppose."

"Let's celebrate the two who are getting married today instead, shall we?"

"If you think that's best, but I am going to still pray that the goot Lord will change Jesse's mind and bring him back home where he belongs. It is so hard, losing Samuel then having Jesse leave. Now Rachel . . ." She looked around, wondering if her daughter had finished tying up the horse. She had told her not to dawdle, but it would be like her to slip in and try to sit with her friends who were also going through their Rumspringa. They were not good influences on her daughter, and she worried every time she saw them together that they would encourage her to leave home. Her heart would break if she lost another child.

Ah, there she was. She raised her hand to beckon to her daughter, but Rachel appeared not to have seen her and walked toward two of her young friends

"Rachel. You will sit with your family." Esther's voice cut through the air. "You know the rules. You have not joined the church yet, and you are not an adult. You do not go off on your own but sit with family at a wedding or any church service."

Rachel's shoulders slumped, and she shot Esther a dark look, but she fell in behind as they went through the barn doors and took their places inside, the bride and groom sitting with the rest of the congregation.

Esther tried to keep her mind on the sermon the bishop gave for well over an hour, but somehow, she only heard little bits and pieces. Finally, a few songs were sung, and the bride and groom came forward to take their vows. Now they only needed to get through the part where anyone in the congregation who wanted to exhort the couple on marriage and family could stand and do so. Her mind drifted back to the day she and Samuel were married, almost thirty-four years ago. She would probably be a widow the rest of her life, and her heart hurt thinking of being alone after her children were all gone from home. Of course, Levi and Sarah would move into her house once Rachel was gone, and they would build her a small Dawdi house on the property, where she would be looked after, but she'd always imagined living there with her Samuel.

She shot a look across the aisle at Daniel Trotter, also a widower for a few years longer than she. Why had he not married again by now? It was common for an Amish man to find a younger wife if he was widowed early, but he never had. Something to think about, for sure and for certain.

Daniel turned his head and met her gaze, and for some reason, she couldn't seem to drop hers. A warm smile lit his face, and he gave a small nod before turning his attention back to the front.

Why was her heart beating so fast? She placed her hand over it to still its thumping. Might there be hope for her future after all? Daniel was a goot, honorable man, and she would be blessed if he chose her as his wife.

Jesse shifted on the hard, backless wooden bench, having forgotten that Amish wedding ceremonies could extend far beyond the two-hour mark—more than one had exceeded three. Hopefully, they'd be finished soon, and he could pick up April.

His mind drifted to April and the lost opportunity last night to ask her to marry him. Had she jumped up because she thought she saw a shooting star, or had she guessed what he was planning and didn't want to give him an answer? Maybe he was rushing her since they'd only been dating six months. No matter how hard Maam tried to convince him that Naomi was the right match for him, his heart knew better. He'd never met such an intelligent, kind, and sweet woman as April. It amazed him how kind she'd been to Maam when she'd been treated with hostility and something almost akin to scorn.

As he gazed at his younger brother and his lovely bride as they stood before the congregation, having been joined as man and wife, he knew he wouldn't have missed this time if he'd had to sit on these benches for another two hours. It was good to be home, at last.

Chapter Twelve

APRIL WALKED INTO THE OFFICE AT the Sunflower Inn where Tabby sat working at her computer. "I need a second opinion. Do you have a minute?" She stopped and then slowly turned, wondering if it had been wise to accept Mrs. Hardin's offer of her dress. She still didn't know what had made Jesse's mom change her mind at the last minute, but at least she wouldn't stand out quite so much as if she'd worn the flowered number with the scoop neck she'd brought for the wedding. "Do I look ridiculous, or just a little silly, or maybe okay?"

Tabby pushed to her feet and walked forward. "It fits you like it was made for you. You said this was Jesse's mother's dress?"

"Yes, but apparently it's been in the closet for years, and she rarely wore it."

"I think you look fantastic. Truly." She turned, opened a closet door, and rummaged around in a box on the floor. "I hope you don't mind. This is from the lost and found, but it's just what you need to make the picture complete." She held out a white prayer capp.

April stepped forward and Tabby slipped it on her head, allowing the strings to dangle loose. "Wow. I can't believe I'm wearing this. Could you take a picture for me to send to my sister?"

"Sure." Tabby took April's phone, snapped a couple of photos, and then handed it back. "You ready for this?"

April took a moment to look at the pictures and then sent a quick text to May. "I think so, as much as I can be."

A ping sounded. May must have been haunting her phone waiting to hear from her. April smiled as she read the message.

"What did she say?" Tabby stepped closer and smiled.

April held up the phone with a laugh. "She said that I look like I've joined the Amish, but if I need rescuing, to send her a text, and she'll come running."

Tabby nodded. "Have you ever thought about that? You and Jesse getting married and joining the church?"

April thought for a long moment but then slowly shook her head. "I don't think I could.

I'm not sure what I'd do if Jesse decided to do that. I mean, the Amish believe in God and all, but I think our faith is too different to blend. It wouldn't be an easy adjustment. From what I understand, they take much of their direction from their bishop rather than going directly to the Bible for themselves. I'll admit, since medical school, I haven't been as faithful to my beliefs as I need to be, and after this trip, that's going to change. I need to find my strength from the Word, not from what a man tells me I should do, even if he says that's based on what God told him."

"That makes sense to me. Do you have any idea how Jesse feels about it all? Do you think there's any chance he'd want to return?"

"I don't. Last night he said he wanted to ask me something, and we got interrupted. I'm kind of afraid that's what he was going to say. He hinted that he's been a bit homesick, that he didn't realize how much he'd given up when he left home." She rubbed her hands up and down her arms, not liking the pit that was hollowing out her stomach. "I kind of didn't want him to talk about it, so I told him I was tired and went to bed."

Tabby looked out the window. "It looks like

the Amish prince is here with his carriage to get Cinderella. You ready to go?"

April nodded, trying to quell the butterflies forming in her stomach now and filling that hole with activity and fluttering up a storm. What would Jesse think of the way she was dressed? She followed Tabby outside, taking a moment to grab a light jacket.

As she walked out, Jesse jumped down from the buggy and walked toward her, admiration lighting his eyes. He looked her over from her prayer capp to her sensible, slip-on shoes. "Who are you, and what have you done with my girlfriend?"

April whirled in a circle, the butterflies starting to settle. "I could say the same about you. You look very handsome. And Amish."

He walked close and held out his arm. "Is that Maam's dress?"

"Yes. Nice, right? Do you like it?"

"Absolutely. But I thought the two of you weren't getting along."

"Well . . . that's kind of a long story. I'll tell you about it after Tabby takes a picture of us in the buggy and we get on the road. I want you to drive this time. We need to get there faster than

I'm willing to drive." She climbed up onto her seat and leaned into him as he settled onto his.

Tabby stepped close, took several shots, and then handed April her phone. "Have fun, kids."

A few minutes later, after traveling at a fast trot the entire way, they pulled up in the yard behind the Hardins' barn where a large number of Amish guests, from toddlers to older couples with white hair, mingled and chatted.

Jesse led the horse over to a waiting man who took it to unharness and turn out into the pasture. Then he came back and joined April. He led her over to greet Levi and Sarah. She extended a hand to Sarah. "Congratulations, you look so lovely."

Sarah ignored her hand and pulled April into a hug. "You are almost my sister, ya? Handshakes are for strangers, not for family."

Warmth filled April, and the butterflies completely disappeared. It was definitely going to be a good day.

Jesse whispered in her ear. "I'll be right back. Just be a minute."

Levi grinned at April. "Look at you. You're a proper Amish woman now, aren't you." He reached out and gave her a one-armed hug.

Sarah giggled. "Next thing you know, she'll be joining the church."

April knew Sarah was teasing, but still . . . She smiled. "One step at a time, folks."

"Lovely dress, April."

April swung around.

Naomi eyed her dress and capp with her brows raised. "Where did you find that?"

Naomi's father and Mrs. Hardin moved up beside her before April had a chance to answer. She inwardly cringed, wondering if Jesse's mom had time to regret her decision in loaning April the dress.

Naomi smirked. "Not bad for an Englischer."

"I had a little help." April bit her lip and chanced a glance at Mrs. Hardin.

Naomi must have seen it as she turned and stared. "Esther. This is your dress?"

Esther seemed to hesitate a few seconds. "Yes. It is." She turned her full gaze on April. "I believe it suits you, April."

April wanted to hug the woman, but she guessed that would be taking things too far. Best to accept it graciously and not make a big deal of it—but what had happened to make her suddenly kind? "Thank you. It's very lovely."

Now if her kindness would last, April could truly enjoy the rest of her time here.

Jesse hurried back over in time to see Naomi's mouth hanging open.

April smiled.

Jesse looked from one to the other, not quite seeming to follow what he'd missed. "Hey, we've almost got a team together for volleyball, but we need more players." He grabbed April's hand. "You in?"

"Volleyball?" She'd seen the nets but hadn't really given it much thought.

"Yep. A traditional Amish pastime. Especially at weddings."

"Well then, when in Amish country . . ." She let Jesse pull her over to the improvised court in the pasture right beyond the area where a large number of buggies were parked. April glanced over her shoulder at Naomi, wondering if she'd follow, but she saw the woman place her hand over her stomach and wince. Should she check on her, or would Naomi even allow it? Jesse's tug at her hand was the deciding vote, and April jogged to the field, excited to be part of the fun.

An Amish teen waved a hand in the air. "Jesse's on our team!"

Rachel planted her fists on her hips. "No way. He's my brother."

"I don't care. I called him first."

April turned to Jesse. "What are you, some kind of Olympic volleyball player or something?"

"Nah. They're just messing around. I have fun at it, but that's about all. I'm surprised they even remember since it's been at least two years since I played with any of them."

"Hmm. I guess we'll see then, won't we?" April got into position near Rachel, and Jesse joined the teen boy on the other side of the net.

Rachel served the ball, and no sooner had it sailed over the net, Jesse jumped up in the air and spiked it, straight down into the ground close to April. The rest of his team shouted, giving each other high-fives.

April glared in mock fury. "Not that good, huh? Game on, buddy. Game on."

Jesse's team served, but the young man who'd begged for Jesse to be on his team lobbed the ball straight into the net, and the entire team groaned.

April grinned. Maybe this wouldn't be such a mismatched game, after all. Twenty minutes later, the game was tied. This time the Amish teen was up for the serve again, and April was ready after it had been volleyed once and Jesse spiked it over the net. She doubled her fists and got under the ball, popping it back over. Another girl on Jesse's team sent it back again, and April jumped as high as she was able and slammed it, driving the ball straight toward the ground. Jesse did a dive into the ground, getting it into the air before it hit, and another young man spiked it, barely out of anyone's reach on April's team, scoring the winning point for Jesse's team.

The team erupted in cheers, and April bent over, clutching her knees and breathing hard. She hadn't had this kind of exercise—or fun—in way too long.

Jesse high-fived the boy who'd missed the first serve but helped them win the game with that final spike. "Great job, everyone."

Rachel patted April on the back. "We'll win the next one."

Jesse approached the net. "Rematch?"

April shook her head. "Haven't you had enough?"

Jesse threw back his head and hooted with laughter. "What? I'm just getting warmed up." He took a towel Naomi handed him and wiped the sweat from his eyes and face and handed it back, giving her a sweet smile.

Naomi stepped closer and dabbed at a spot on his forehead, her eyes gazing into his.

Someone laughed and dashed in front of April, snapping her out of the desire to step forward and say something to Naomi she'd probably regret—or to grab that towel out of her hand and fling it as far as she could. She was a guest here, and she shouldn't make a scene, even if she didn't appreciate the way Naomi was acting toward *her* boyfriend. She waited a few minutes to allow herself to calm down, grateful when Naomi sauntered away. "Ready, April?" Rachel touched April's arm."

"I think I need a cup of water first. Give me five minutes, okay? Anyone else want water?"

Several voices called out, "Me."

April waved and headed for the table where water was being served. As she approached the table, her spirits sank. Of all the people who had to be standing there, why couldn't it be someone other than Naomi? The young woman had beamed at Jesse anytime he'd looked her direction during the game and seemed to look down her nose at April an equal number of times. At least Mrs. Hardin had shared she'd loaned the dress to her rather than humiliating her by saying Rachel had taken it out of the closet without permission to give to April. She shuddered at the memory of that earlier confrontation in Mrs. Hardin's bedroom the day before.

She pulled a wicker tray from a stack and placed a half-dozen paper cups on it. She started to fill each one with water from the five-gallon jug with a spigot at the base. Feeling Naomi's eyes on her she turned. "Did you want one too?" April tried to keep her voice light and friendly, as there was no need to make a scene.

"Nein. You appear to be quite thirsty. Are you drinking all of that yourself?" A small smirk pulled at Naomi's lips.

"No. Several of the team asked me to bring them a glass as well." She set the last one on the tray, prepared to get out of Naomi's presence as soon as possible. "Jesse did well, don't you think? He's an amazing volleyball player." She had no idea why those words flew from her mouth—she did not want to engage this woman in conversation, and especially not about Jesse of all people. But the hand Naomi put on her abdomen and the small wince made her decide to stay a minute longer.

"There is much you don't know about

Jesse, his family, his upbringing." Naomi raised her head and huffed.

"I know you and Jesse have history together from the past. That you've known each other all your lives, and that you used to hope he'd marry you. I also know you married someone else." There. She'd said what she'd been wanting to say for the last few hours.

"Ya." Naomi planted her crossed arms over her chest. "We have known each other our whole lives, while you have known him only a few months, from what his *mudder* says."

"I understand that, Naomi, but he and I are together now. We're dating and I wish—"

Naomi moved into April's personal space, her eyes narrowed. "It wasn't until our teens that Jesse began to question his beliefs—to question what he wanted to do with his life." Naomi's words cut through April's as though she hadn't spoken. "To wonder if all of this was enough." She waved her hand toward the barn and the farmland.

"I understand that. He's shared that with me, but people change, Naomi. Things don't always stay the same. People grow up, and they often start wanting something different." She picked up the tray and took a step.

"Do you *really* understand?" Naomi gave a soft snort of derision. "You can wear an Amish dress, ride in an Amish buggy, even learn to drive one, and eat all the Amish food that's set before you. That doesn't change anything—it doesn't make you one of us." She gestured toward the grassy area where the players were lounging. She waved at Jesse, and April was dismayed to see him wave back and smile. "He can change what he wears, how he talks, where he lives, but it doesn't mean he's one of you—that he's not still Amish inside. I've seen the way he looks since he got back—the homesickness on his face when he thinks no one is looking."

April pursed her lips, knowing she might cry if she opened them to reply, but Naomi went on as though she didn't really want a reply. "Tell me you don't see it. The way he laughs with his friends and family. The Englisch life he's chosen won't last. Neither will you. He'll come back to us—where he belongs."

April blinked away tears and cleared her throat. "You're wrong, Naomi. Dead wrong."

Naomi simply smiled and raised one brow. "Am I? Are you sure of that?" She stood for a few seconds, as though waiting for an answer this time. Then she wrapped her arm across her abdomen again and pain flashed across her face. She gave a small moan and then straightened. "Even if I am wrong, you'll never be welcome here. If you marry him, you'll drive him away. He won't be able to come home because of you. You'll only drive him farther away from the people and the life he really loves, and he'll soon come to resent you for it." She started to turn and walk away, but she grabbed her middle with both arms and doubled over, a groan of pain ripping through the air.

Chapter Thirteen

April stepped forward, her doctor's instinct kicking into high gear. "Naomi. What's wrong?"

Several people must have heard the repeated groans, as Esther, Daniel, Jesse, and a few others moved closer. April grabbed a nearby chair and placed it behind Naomi. She reached for Naomi's arm. "Sit down. What's happening? Talk to me."

Naomi didn't seem to hear April or see the chair. She wobbled sideways and then toppled over onto the grass. Her father knelt beside her, stroking her arm, his face contorted as he looked up at April. "You are a doctor? What is wrong with her?"

Rachel, Sarah, and Levi raced over and stopped at the sight of Naomi writhing on the ground. Rachel sidled over to her mother. "Maam?" Her voice came out in a loud whisper. "Is she going to die like Daed did?"

April barely registered the words, but she saw Esther put her arm around the girl's shoulders and draw her close. April looked up. "Not if I can help it." She knelt down beside Naomi and touched her arm. "Naomi. You need to describe the pain you're feeling. Tell me what's going on. I can't help you if you don't tell me."

Naomi moaned again and put her hand over her abdomen. "It feels like someone has shoved a knife in here. A sharp pain. I can barely breath. Oh, it hurts so much now."

"Has this happened before?"

"Ya. A little yesterday, but only a twinge or two. Then this morning, it started again" She winced and clutched at her side. "Then it got much, much worse."

April leaned over. "I'm going to put my hand on your belly and press down. Tell me what hurts more, when I press down or when I take the pressure off, okay?"

Naomi nodded.

April put her hand over the spot and pressed. Naomi winced, but as soon as April released the pressure, she emitted a short scream. "That was very, very bad."

April rocked back on her heels. "That gives me my answer."

Esther elbowed her way forward. "What are

you doing to her, causing her more pain? You must stop that this minute."

"She has appendicitis." April held out her hand to Jesse, and he pulled her to her feet. "She needs to get to the hospital immediately."

Jesse pulled a phone from his pocket and stared dialing. "I'm on it. You stay with her." He stepped away, and April could hear his voice quietly requesting an ambulance.

Whispers in the crowd increased, and April could hear grumbles and questions. Would these people stop Naomi from getting the help she needed? She whirled around, ready to defend her decision when Daniel Trotter placed his hand on her arm. "Dr. Monroe has said my daughter needs help, and I trust her that she knows what she's doing. We will wait for the ambulance since taking her by buggy might cause her too much pain. Please, just pray for my Naomi, and let the doctor do her job."

The crowd quieted, and April saw several people nod and start to move away. She glanced at Daniel and then over at Mrs. Hardin. The older woman was kneeling beside Naomi, murmuring words of comfort to the younger woman she'd planned for her son to marry one day.

April moved aside a few minutes later when an ambulance siren sounded out at the road and came into view as it sped up the drive not long after. She stepped over to the EMTs as they pulled out a gurney and brought it and their medical bags to the prone woman. April explained her credentials and her findings as she walked beside them.

One of the men who appeared to be in his early thirties nodded as he knelt beside Naomi. "Good call, Doc. Glad you were here. We don't get many calls from this part of the community. Too few, in fact. She's lucky you were around, or it could have been a lot worse."

"You'll get her straight to surgery?"

"Yes. We'll put a call in to the hospital with your findings and our stats as soon as we load her in the bus. They'll be prepping and ready when she arrives. She's in good hands."

"Thank you." April watched as they loaded Naomi into the ambulance.

Daniel walked alongside the gurney. He turned to Esther. "I'm going with her and will wait until she's out of surgery. I am sorry for the disruption to the wedding." He bowed his head briefly.

Esther reached out and touched his hand.

"Please, don't worry. Go, be with your daughter. Gott be with you both. I will pray for her and for you."

April watched Jesse as he stood next to her, Naomi's last words racing through her mind and refusing to leave. Would she destroy any chance of lasting happiness Jesse might have if they stayed together and eventually married? She couldn't even look him in the eyes right now, or she knew he'd see into her heart.

"Hey?" He brushed a strand of hair off her forehead, his touch sending a shiver through her that she didn't want to acknowledge. "Are you all right?"

She shrugged. "Of course. It's Naomi you should be asking about, not me." She turned her head a fraction, and he dropped his hand.

"She'll be okay, I assume? I know appendicitis is very treatable nowadays, but I'm still very proud of you, the way you jumped in, diagnosed it, and convinced Daniel to let the ambulance come get her. She might not have been all right, otherwise."

"Thanks."

"April?" He touched her chin and turned her face toward him. "What is it?"

"I don't know. Just . . ." She sighed. "I'm fine."

The EMT stepped toward them as the driver shut the back doors. "Thanks again for your help, doctor. We're heading out now. We'll take good care of her and her father."

April held up her hand. "Wait. I want to come with you. Make sure she's okay."

The man hesitated but nodded. "I guess that's all right. There's no room in the back with her father there, but you can sit up front, if you don't mind."

"Sure. Yes." She started to follow.

Jesse grabbed her hand. "Hey! What's going on. You said she'd be fine, so what's up with you suddenly thinking you need to go?"

She pivoted and finally met his gaze. "I can't stay here, Jesse." She reached up and removed the prayer capp. "I'm going to call my sister to come get me. I'll leave your mother's dress with Tabby at the B&B. I'm sorry."

"What? You're breaking up with me?" He reached out like he wanted to take her in his arms, but she backed away two steps.

"I'll never be accepted here, Jesse. You know that, and I know that. Your mother didn't like me even before she met me. Your sister and brother have been kind, but that doesn't mean I'd be accepted by the community if we were ever to marry. I'd hold you back from your people. From this life." She waved her hand in the air. "I don't want you to end up resenting me, and I don't want to come between you and your family. That would never work."

"No! I don't agree. This isn't the way I want things to be. Not now or ever." He took another step toward her, and she glanced over her shoulder to see the ambulance starting. "I have to go, Jesse. I really believe that in the long run we're better off if we end it now, so there's no more hurt or expectations."

"Wait a minute. I wanted to marry you. I was going to propose the other night on the porch when you thought you saw a shooting star. I love you!" He reached into his pocket and pulled out a ring box, opened it and shoved it toward her. "See? I'm serious about this. I don't want you to leave. Please, April?" His eyes were pleading, and she could see tears welling there as he must have taken in the truth shining from her eyes.

April turned her head so he wouldn't see the tears that started to fall. "Coming!" She shouted over her shoulder to the EMT who beckoned for her to come. "I'm sorry, Jesse. Truly I am." She dashed for the open passenger door of the ambulance and climbed in, not daring to look back at the man she loved with all of her heart—and who's heart she knew she'd break if she accepted his proposal.

Chapter Fourteen

Jesse stood there watching the ambulance disappear down the long driveway, taking his heart with it. He wasn't even sure what had happened in the last few minutes. What had made April walk away like that, without even taking the time to talk things through? She'd mentioned she knew his mother didn't like her even before she arrived. Had Maam said something more that he wasn't aware of? Had she overheard Maam and Daniel discussing the two of them, or had Naomi said something before she collapsed.

Whatever it was, he had to get to the bottom of this. He loved that girl, and no way did he want to lose her. He stared at the ring box still clutched in his hand. Not even seeing the ring and knowing his intent had swayed April's decision to leave. He pulled out his phone and tried calling, praying she'd be willing to take the time to talk before calling her sister. It rang three times but dropped into voicemail.

He strode toward the house, not sure what he planned to do but knowing he couldn't allow this to happen. He drew to a sudden halt. There were still more than half of the wedding guests here, and a few were watching him and probably wondering what was going on. He couldn't barge into the house now and demand an answer from Maam. Naomi wasn't here, and her father was with her. His shoulders sagged. As much as he hated the thought, he'd have to wait until everyone went home. He didn't want to destroy the joy of this day for his brother and his new wife. That wouldn't be fair, and it certainly wouldn't be what April would expect from him. Somehow, he'd have to pretend that all was well until he could discuss this privately with his family.

Later that evening, after unsuccessfully trying April's phone at least a dozen times with no answer, he put his fork down next to his shoofly pie without taking more than a bite.

Rachel sank down on a chair beside him on the front porch. "What's wrong? Did a real fly land on it?" She poked him in the ribs and laughed. She sobered when he didn't join her. "I've never seen you ignore a piece of pie before. What happened? I know April went to the hospital with Naomi, which was very kind of her, but why isn't she back? Is that why you're so sad?"

"Guess I'm not too hungry." He held out the plate. "You want it?"

"It's not bad, is it?" She eyed him for a long moment. "What's going on, Jesse? Where's April? Aren't you going to pick her up and bring her back for dessert?"

"No." He might as well get it over with. They'd all know soon enough, anyway. "She left."

"For the inn? Was she too tired to come back? I saw you on the phone a couple of times. What did she say? She'll be here tomorrow, right, so we can all say good-bye?"

"No. She left for New York. Without me. Her sister is coming to get her. I'm not sure when or what she's doing, because she won't take my calls. She ended things. It's over."

"What?" Rachel nearly spit out the bite of pie she'd taken. "That can't be true. I can tell she likes you a lot. She's gone? Really, truly gone? Why?"

"She thinks I'm better off without her—that it would have happened sooner or later, so it was better not to drag things out." He buried his face in his hands.

A step sounded nearby, and a warm hand landed on his shoulder. Levi. "I don't think Maam's lack of hospitality helped, brudder. I'm afraid she wasn't always kind to April."

Jesse's heart warmed at his brother's championship of April, but the old need to defend his family that he'd felt as a young boy rose up almost in spite of himself. "I don't want to blame Maam."

Rachel hmphed. "I do. I mean, it's not *not* her fault, entirely. She never made April feel welcome."

"That's kind of you, Jesse," Levi said. "I'll pray for you, brudder. I hear Sarah calling, so I'd better go. But remember that we love you."

"Thank you, Levi. That means a lot." Jesse raised his head and looked at Rachel. "April said Maam let her wear her dress today."

Rachel rolled her eyes. "Ya. After making her feel terrible for even thinking about it, and after scolding me for suggesting it. She was against April before she came, all because she was so sure and certain Naomi was the right woman for you."

Jesse gripped the arms of his chair, wishing

he could find a way to change all of this. "I planned to propose to April. I shouldn't have waited so long. Maybe if I'd told her sooner that I love her . . . I thought she knew how I felt. I thought she felt the same way. Man, I blew it!"

Rachel stared at him. "Why didn't you? Why would you put off something so important?"

Jesse shook his head, not wanting to go into what happened on the porch of the B&B or that he'd shown April the ring today and she'd still walked away. "It's . . . complicated, Rachel."

She huffed. "Everyone treats me like I'm a little kid. I'm not. I'm almost a woman. I have to make big decisions for myself soon. I wish people would start remembering that."

He considered her words and nodded. "So you are, Rachel. I appreciate the reminder. It's complicated because part of me worried this would happen if I brought April here to meet our family. I didn't know what she'd think of my past life, of all of you." He met her gaze. "She was a thoroughbred about all of it. Even with the way Maam treated her—and probably Naomi too—she was kind and didn't get angry. I see now that it must have hurt her, though. I should have talked to Maam. Should have tried to help April more." He shook his head. "Maybe April was right. I don't know. The longer love lasts, the more it hurts when it ends. That's what she said today. That she was ending it because I'd just get hurt more and end up resenting her because people here wouldn't accept her. If I'd been honest about my Amish roots when I first met her, maybe it would have scared her away—or we never would have dated, I wouldn't have fallen in love, and it wouldn't hurt like it does now."

Rachel leaned close and touched his arm. "Does it have to end? Does it have to hurt? Will it end up being like this with Levi and Sarah, then? Did love end for Maam and Daed? Is that what I have to look forward to, whether I stay Amish or become Englisch? Isn't it better to fall in love than not at all?" Her eyes reflected panic and fear.

Jesse reached out and enclosed her hand in his. "I know Maam and Daed loved each other, and I believe Levi and Sarah do as well. I believe it will last. The Englisch world is . . . different, little sister."

She jerked her hand away. "So there's no real love there, is that what you're saying? Or do you mean that when things get hard, people give up on love and walk away? Is that what April did? Is that the Englisch way, or is it your way? Or April's way?" She glared at him and pushed to her feet.

Maam stepped out on the porch and clapped her hands. "Jesse, Rachel, we need your help. All the guests have gone, but there is still much to put in order before we go to bed. Come. You can't sit out here all evening."

Jesse pushed to his feet, keeping his face turned away, unable to look at his mother right now. He knew he'd say something he'd regret, and that wasn't the Amish way either. He plunged into the house, not caring that his mother was tutting behind him. He'd had enough for one night, and maybe, forever.

Esther looked from the retreating back of her son to the stormy eyes of her daughter and then planted her fists on her hips and glared. "What is wrong with him?"

Rachel appeared to be holding in an angry retort, and Esther realized her own tiredness had made her words come out much sharper than she'd planned. "I'm sorry. Is something wrong, Rachel? With your brudder? This should be a happy day, ya? Levi and Sarah marrying. Is he worried for Naomi?" Her spirits lifted. April hadn't returned after going to the hospital, which was just as well, but she'd been saddened that Jesse hadn't shown enough concern to drive to the hospital to check on Naomi. Which woman was her boy pining for?

"Ha, that is funny, Maam." Rachel's tone didn't match her words, and no humor showed in her narrowed eyes as she turned them on Esther.

"What has gotten into you, daughter?" Esther almost gasped in shock at the disrespect in Rachel's voice.

"You really think he's upset about Naomi?" Rachel shook her head. "April broke up with him and went back to New York. That's what's wrong."

Joy surged through Esther at the news. "April is gone?" She clasped her hands in front of her heart. "That is goot news. Maybe our Naomi will have a chance now."

"Maam! I can't believe you'd say that when Jesse is hurting. He doesn't care about Naomi, other than as a friend. He never did. But you had to keep pushing her at him."

Esther bristled, suddenly alive to the way her daughter was talking to her. "Do not take that tone with me, daughter. I am still your mother."

"Or what, Maam? You'll send me to my room or take a switch to me? I think I'm a little too old for that, don't you? I'm in my Rumspringa, remember? When I can make my own decisions about my life."

Esther gasped at the cold tone in Rachel's voice. "Why are you trying to ruin this wonderful day when your brudder got married? You would take all the joy out of it by your words and actions?"

Rachel shook her head. "You ruined it first, Maam, by the way you treated April and drove her away." She stomped toward the door and didn't look back.

"You do not walk away from me, young lady. I am not done talking to you. You come back out here until I excuse you."

Rachel pivoted and her eyes were colder than Esther had ever seen them. "I'm getting my things, and I'm leaving. I won't be staying here any longer."

"Rachel!" Esther almost shouted the word as her little girl walked into the house without looking back.

Chapter Fifteen

APRIL DIDN'T TRY TO STEM THE tears that rolled down her cheeks. She'd had no idea what to expect out of this brief visit to Jesse's family, but it certainly hadn't been this—leaving him behind and second-guessing herself every minute wondering if she'd made the right decision. If it was only about her, she'd run back and throw her arms around him, letting him know how much she loved him. She could live with knowing his family—or rather, his maam and at least part of the Amish community—would never accept her, but she couldn't do that to Jesse—it just wasn't fair.

She tucked the last few things into her bag and then slumped onto the bed and picked up her phone. She glanced at the screen and froze, completely forgetting she'd changed her background to the photo of her and Jesse in the Amish buggy that Tabby took. She slid it into her pocket, wondering if she should call May again. She'd promised to come, but it was still early in the day. No doubt they'd be another couple of hours, since she'd called after dinner last night.

At that exact moment, the phone rang, causing her to jump off the bed and stumble. Could Jesse be calling again? What would she say if she answered? He'd already tried several times, and she'd let it roll over to voicemail. She peeked at the screen. May. Tapping the screen, she worked to control the waver in her voice. "Hi, May. Are you on your way?"

"Nope. We're not on the way."

April frowned, not sure what her sister was getting at. Had something come up, and they couldn't come after all? "O-kay . . ."

"We're downstairs!"

April heard feet pounding up the stairs, and she flung open the door in time to get caught in a bear hug from her big sister. She sank into the hug for a few seconds and then pulled back. "Thanks. I needed that." She peered over the banister. "Is Rob downstairs?"

"Yep. Drinking what smelled like a fantastic cup of coffee. Tabby offered me one, but I told her I had to come see you first." May glanced at the suitcase on the bed. "All ready to go?"

"I am." April slipped her hand through the

strap and set the bag on the floor, letting the wheels engage as she pulled it to the top of the stairs. They went down in silence, and April appreciated that her sister wasn't peppering her with questions.

As they walked into the kitchen, Rob turned, his brown face and warm smile lighting as she lifted a hand in greeting. "Hey, Rob. Thanks so much for the rescue. The two of you must have left in the wee hours of the morning to get here so early."

He gave a half shrug. "It's no problem. Zack spent the night at a friend's last night, and a neighbor is watching our dog."

May slipped her hand through the crook of April's arm. "Besides, we'd go anywhere that family needs us." She glanced out the window and grinned. "Especially if it's Amish country and Tabby's B&B."

Rob laughed. "I agree. Bring on the pies and goodies. These people know how to cook."

Tabby stepped forward and placed a mug of coffee into April's hands. "Here you go. This will help perk you up this morning. Exactly the way you like it."

"I can't believe you remember preferences

with all the guests you must have." April took a sip. "Hmm. Perfect, thank you."

A few minutes later, April had filled them in on the events leading up to the race to the hospital with Naomi. "After she headed to surgery and I'd spoken to the attending doctor, I took a taxi back here. Tabby was amazing. She sat up with me and listened to me blubber and cry for the first hour. Then she tucked me into bed and told me the best medicine was sleep. I didn't think I'd be able to get some rest, but I did—for nine hours, but I still woke up feeling groggy and half here."

Tabby pushed to her feet, grabbed the coffeepot, and refilled their cups. "Sometimes a girl needs a good cry, and you had plenty of reasons for that last night. I didn't mind at all. That's part of being a good host. To know when to listen."

May reached across the table and covered April's hand. "We're more than happy to take you home, but I'm afraid you're going to end up regretting leaving without really talking this out with Jesse."

Rob nodded. "You're the one who helped convince our families to accept our marriage and stood by us when they couldn't see it. If our parents can change their minds, maybe Jesse's can too."

"I don't know." April hated to argue, but she'd seen the look in Mrs. Hardin's eyes and heard the truth in Naomi's words.

"Why not?" May released her hand and leaned back.

"Because I don't think the Amish change. They're set in their ways. They don't take to Englischers or things they feel don't fit into their world. Family is very important to Jesse, just like it is to me. I won't make him choose between me and his family."

Tabby raised one brow. "It looks like to me you're making his choice for him. Is that fair?"

"It's better this way. It's already painful enough, and this was apt to happen at some point, so getting it out of the way now won't hurt as much."

Chapter Sixteen

Esther Hardin drove her buggy into the hospital parking lot. She looked around, unsure where to leave her horse. They didn't appear to have any hitching rails here, so what should she do? She stopped along the edge of the large lot, not far from the front doors, her heart pounding in fear. She'd never been in the hospital before, and it felt as if a foreign world loomed in front of her, daring her to enter or run. She stiffened her spine. Amish women were not cowards, and she was not an exception, danke very much.

Wrapping the reins around the brake handle that she set goot and hard, she sat for a minute, wondering what to do next. Why was visiting Naomi so frightening? She thought back to the day her Samuel had died at home. If he'd been willing—no—if she'd insisted that he'd come to this place, would he still be alive and with their family today? Wrapping her arms around her middle, she shuddered at the grief and guilt that almost leveled her. Was it her fault he was dead? She bit her lip hard to keep a sob from passing her lips, working to regain her composure. Then she stepped down from the buggy and approached a man wearing white who stood outside the front doors. "Young man?"

"Yes?" He turned and then smiled. "How may I help you, ma'am?"

A polite Englischer. This was nice. She gave a quick nod. "I parked my buggy there, but the reins are only looped around the brake. Martha—my mare—she's getting old and not apt to try to run away, but will it be safe to leave her, do you think?"

"I can keep an eye on her if you'd like. I was raised on a farm, and I'm familiar with horses. I'm out here for my break, and I'm not due in for another fifteen minutes. If you think you'll be longer than that, I can get permission to stay a little longer."

She shook her head. "Nein. No. I will not be longer. Danke. Thank you." She felt it only right she speak in words he could understand after the kindness he was showing. "That is very kind of you." She walked with steady purpose to the doors and hesitated, glancing back over her shoulder. The young man smiled again and nodded once more. Squaring her shoulders, she reached out to push the door, but it whooshed open, making her start. Of course, they had these doors in a couple of the stores she frequented, but these were large and fast, and she hadn't quite been ready for the quiet efficiency.

Inside, a small area of chairs, a few end tables, and a desk in the corner, bespoke this was a waiting area for people who had folks they cared for in this place. A gray-haired woman wearing glasses sat at the desk typing something into a computer. She looked up as Esther approached, scanning her attire from her capp to the hem of her dress. Of course, the woman probably saw very few Amish come through these doors. "May I help you?" A warm smile lit her face.

Esther released the breath she hadn't realized she'd been holding. "Ya. I'm here to see Naomi Trotter. She was admitted yesterday evening."

The receptionist typed for a moment and then looked up. "Yes. She's on the second floor. Room 3B. Would you like me to show you the way?"

"If you would be so kind. Danke." Esther felt humbled at yet another kind Englischer going out of the way to help.

After a quick ride in an elevator and a walk down a hall, the receptionist tapped on a door and then stepped aside. "She's right in here, and she's allowed another visitor, so you're welcome to go on in. I'll get back to my desk now. You can find your way out?"

"I can. Thank you." Esther stepped into the room, her gaze landing on Daniel sitting in a chair next to Naomi's bed. The young woman's bed was elevated about a foot above the level point, and her capp was missing from her head, with her blond hair still in a braid and laying across her shoulder. She was clothed in a print hospital gown and her skin was pale, almost ashen.

Daniel rose to his feet as she entered. "Esther. How goot of you to come. Danke." He grasped the back of another chair and pulled it beside his, offering her a seat before he sat next to her.

Esther reached out and touched Naomi's hand. "I'm sorry for not bringing you anything, but since you just had surgery and seemed in so much pain, I wasn't sure bringing food would be welcome. How are you feeling, my dear? We were all so worried about you."

"A little tired, and the incision still hurts, but they've given me something to help with that." She gingerly touched the place on her side covered by a white sheet and a light blanket. "The pain I was in before is gone, though, so that's wunderbar."

Daniel beamed. "The doctor said she may be able to come home this afternoon or tomorrow morning. He's making his rounds right after lunch, and he'll decide then."

"So soon?" Esther had trouble comprehending such a thing. "Didn't you have surgery? How could they send you home so soon?"

"Ya, she did, but the doctor said this is a very common, safe surgery. Naomi will be sore and needs to take it easy for several weeks, with no lifting or any strenuous exercise, but she'll be fine. It is amazing to me as well. These Englisch doctors are miracle workers. I'm sorry I refused to ever consider allowing my family to see a doctor before."

Naomi shifted on the bed as though trying to get comfortable. "Esther, can you tell me where April is, please? Is she still at your house or back at the Sunflower Inn?"

Esther raised her chin, happy to be able to impart such good news to this young woman she cared for so much. "You will be glad to know she has gone back to New York. Alone. She broke up with Jesse and left."

Naomi uttered a soft moan and tears filled her eyes.

Daniel reached out and grabbed her hand. "Shall I call for a nurse? Are you in pain again?"

"Nein." Naomi shook her head and reached for a tissue box next to her bed, pulling one out and dabbing at her eyes. "I feel horrible, but not in physical pain. At the reception yesterday, I said some horrible things to April. Hateful things that I realize now weren't true. They were lies, all of them. I was so jealous of her. Every time Jesse looked at her, I could see how much he loved her. What I said may have driven her away. I owe her an apology." She buried her face in her hands and sniffed.

Esther sat stunned, barely able to take in what she was hearing. Naomi was taking responsibility for April leaving her Jesse? But . . . she had always believed Naomi and Jesse were meant to be together. "What does this mean, Naomi? You love Jesse, too. He can still come to care for you now that April is gone. I'm sure of it."

Naomi sniffed harder. "But that's just it. I thought I was in love with him, but now I realize it was left over from our childhood. I loved my husband, and I still miss him." The tears flowed now in earnest, and she reached for another tissue. "I need to tell April I'm sorry. I was wrong to interfere. If she hadn't been there and helped me, even after the ugly things I said to her, who knows what would have happened. I might have died." She covered her face with the wad of tissue and wept, her shoulders shaking.

"There, there, little one, don't cry." Daniel raised tired eyes and met Esther's gaze.

She pushed to her feet and took a step away from the chair. "The doctor said Naomi needs to rest, so I should be going. I am so sorry for your distress, but I'm glad you'll be going home soon. We'll bring food by the house tomorrow. We will pray for you, too." She dipped her head in silent prayer and then strode to the door, Naomi's words of self-recrimination nearly driving her to run back to her buggy. What was she to do with this new information? How could she take in the change in Naomi's feelings and her own goals for this young woman and her son? She nearly sprinted down the hall to the elevator but passed it by and took the stairs, glad to have something to do to help burn off the horrible feelings rising inside.

Esther climbed into the buggy, barely remembering to thank the nice man who had watched over her horse. She flicked her reins and sent Martha into a faster gait than she typically moved, intent on finding her daughter. She'd lost one child already, and she suddenly knew that if something didn't change soon, she would lose a second one as well. Rachel loved to go to the general store and visit with her friends. Rachel didn't know her maam knew that, but Esther had her sources.

She pulled into the parking area and spotted her girl sitting on the porch between an Amish boy and girl who both wore Englischer clothing, and they were all looking at the boy's phone.

Rachel looked up as Esther pulled Martha to a halt. Her daughter bolted from her chair and headed for the front door, her friends following.

"Rachel. Wait. Please." Esther dropped the reins and climbed from the buggy as her girl paused while the other two went through the door. Seeming to regret her inaction, she reached for the door and pulled it open. Esther stopped at the bottom step. "Please, Rachel. Allow me a minute to talk to you. Then if you still want to leave after that, I won't try to stop you."

Rachel waited with her hand on the door. Then she slowly released the handle and turned. "All right. A minute. That's all."

"Danke. I have just come from talking to Naomi at the hospital. She is doing better, and she may even come home today."

Rachel narrowed her eyes. "You can thank April for that. Her quick thinking and correct diagnosis are what saved Naomi's life."

"Ya. I know. I plan to do that very thing."

A shocked expression passed quickly over Rachel's face but then disappeared as her expression shuttered into a blank stare.

Esther pressed on, hoping Rachel would hear her out. "You asked why I dislike Englischers. I do not dislike them all, but I dislike what they stand for. I know there are goot people among the Englisch. I guess I shouldn't even say I dislike what they stand for, as many have good moral standards, even if they live differently from us—but they took my

Jesse from me. Then seeing your interest in the Englisch world now that you're in your Rumspringa, I have been so fearful I would lose another child. I lay awake at night, praying, worrying, crying, hoping it will not be so, but lately, I fear that the things I have done will drive you away and make you choose their life, not ours."

Rachel's eyes widened, and she placed her fingers over her mouth. "Maam . . ."

"Nein." Esther held up her hand. "I must finish before you speak." She softened her tone, realizing she had spoken harshly again. "I am sorry. Forgive me. I need to tell you the rest, please."

Rachel nodded.

"The truth is, you are not a child. You have always been a level-headed person, even as a young girl. I always trusted you and never worried. Now, in trying to keep you close to me, to keep you from leaving our home, I fear I have driven you away. I was wrong in what I said a minute ago. The Englisch didn't take Jesse. He made his own choice because of his love for animals and his desire to doctor them. I realize now he made the right decision for him, even if not for me. I am so sorry that I did not trust you to make the right decision for your path in life. Whatever you decide, whether it be to stay with us or go out into the Englisch world, I will always love you, and I will support you. No matter what." She waited, trying to read Rachel's somber expression, but her face didn't soften. Esther turned, walked to the horse, and reached up to grab the handrail and pull herself up.

"Maam?" Rachel's wide eyes drove a spike right into Esther's heart. Was her girl finally ready to make her decision to leave the faith? Had her confession of wrong doing come too late to make a difference in her young life?

She placed her hand over her heart, willing it to calm its wild beating and praying she could accept whatever might be coming. "Ya?"

"Wait. Please." Rachel raced down the stairs and threw herself into Esther's arms. After a long time holding each other, Rachel pulled back. "Do you think I could get a ride home with you? I want to stay there now, if it's okay."

Esther nodded and smiled. "Ya. I would like that very much."

Chapter Seventeen

JESSE STOOD ON THE FRONT PORCH of the farmhouse he'd called home for his first eighteen years as bittersweet memories washed over him, as well as a boat-load of regret. How would his life have differed if he'd never left this place? Would he have married a sweet Amish girl and have one or two children by now? It hurt to think of never having met April, but neither of them would have been so deeply wounded if he'd stayed. He set down his suitcase as the rest of his family surged through the door.

Rachel reached out and threw her arms around him in a gigantic hug. "I don't want you to leave. I'll miss you so much." She buried her face against his shoulder, and he felt warm tears dampen his shirt.

He patted her shoulder and then drew back. "I'll miss you even more." He ran the back of his hand down her cheek and tweaked her chin. "I'm glad you decided to come home."

She nodded. "Me too. I think this is where I belong."

Levi clapped a hand on Jesse's back. "Don't stay away so long next time, brudder. It might be a while before we have another wedding, so you must come before then."

"I'll be sure of that, Levi." He nodded to Sarah. "Keep this one in line, and don't let him make too much trouble."

She smiled and dipped her head. "I'll try."

"Maam." He turned to his mother but didn't hold out his arms. He knew he should, but it still rankled that April had left so abruptly, and Maam had been a part of the reason.

She stepped forward, her eyes shadowed, and thrust an envelope into his hands. "Take this. It's something I should have given you long ago. I am so sorry now that I didn't. It's yours."

Jesse held it up and shock coursed through his body. He'd recognize this handwriting anywhere. He raised his eyes and met his mother's. "Daed wrote me a letter?"

"Ya." She twisted her hands together and bit her lip.

He didn't wait for her to say more but ripped it open and withdrew the single sheet of paper covered in his father's spidery handwriting.

Jesse,

It has been a long time since we've spoken, but I have put this off too long. I need you to know that I am so proud of all you have accomplished. Maam tells me you have started work at an animal hospital in New York. While it is true that I have never really understood your need to leave to live among the Englisch, it is clear that Gott has a plan for your life that is outside of our small community. I want you to know that I love you, son, even if I'm often too proud or stubborn to tell you. Please forgive me for the things that have come between us in the past.

Your daed,
Samuel Hardin

His mother took a step toward him but halted, her eyes filling with tears. "I'm so sorry, Jesse. I should have given you this after your father died. I should have told you that he was proud of you and loved you instead of allowing you to think he was angry that you decided to leave us. I should have told you that I love you and am proud of you, too. Can you ever forgive me?"

He drew in a long breath, and all the anger and hurt from the past years seemed to leave with his exhale. God had forgiven him multiple times and often for more than this. How could he possibly deny his forgiveness to the woman who had given him life? He reached out and drew her into his arms and then gave her a long hug. "Yes. Of course, I forgive you." After a few seconds, he released her and stepped back. "But there's someone else you need to ask as well."

She nodded and swiped at a tear rolling down her cheek. "Ya. I know."

Esther squeezed her son's hand and sniffed one last time. "Please. Would you give me a few minutes before you leave?"

A slight V formed between his brows as he looked at her. Then he gave a slow nod. "Sure. I can do that."

She reached out and grabbed Rachel's hand. "Come, daughter. I will need your help."

Rachel's eyes widened, but she didn't resist as Esther led her into the house and to Esther's bedroom. "I need to pack quickly, but I'm too flustered to think straight. Do you have a suitcase I can use? How much clothing will I need for a couple of days in New York City?"

Rachel placed her hand over her mouth and smothered a gasp. "You're going to New York with Jesse?"

"Ya. I haven't told him yet, but how else would I get there to talk to April if not to ride with my son?" She planted her hands on her hips but smiled. "So. Are you going to stand here talking, or do you have something I can put clothing into?"

Rachel's mouth dropped at Esther's words. She snapped it shut. "I'll go get it. Wait right here." Rapid footsteps disappeared down the hall and a door slammed shut a few moments later. Then the footsteps padded back to Esther's door. Rachel rushed in and slung a suitcase onto the bed. "Here it is. How can I help?"'

"Hmm. I think maybe two dresses, a warm sweater and maybe a coat, plus the necessary underthings? You find the dresses, and I'll get the rest." She looked down at her sensible shoes. "These will be all right?" She looked up at Rachel. "I know I will stand out among all the many Englischers there, but they are my most comfortable ones." She touched the strings of her capp. "I might want to bring an extra capp as well, ya?"

"Ya." Rachel tossed her a grin and then flung open the closet door. "I'm so excited you want to go. I wish I could come, but I'll take care of things for you here while you're gone. April is going to be so surprised."

"If she will speak to me after the way I treated her—and if she's even there. I suppose Jesse knows where she lives and works, but what if we get there and she's gone somewhere else?" She put her hand to her throat and stared at her daughter who knew so much more about Englisch ways. "Do you think we should try to call her first?"

Rachel shook her head. "Jesse's tried calling and left messages. I know. I heard him this morning, but she never answers her phone. I guess you'll have to go and hope for the best."

"I shall pray, not hope. Gott surely will not deny me the chance to make peace with April after the wrongs I have done her."

"I'll pray too, Maam." Rachel gave her a

quick hug and then turned back to the closet.

"Goot. That will be goot." Warmth spread through Esther's heart as she laid her things in the open suitcase and watched her daughter. Gott *was* good, and He would take care of this thing she had done and help her to set it right. He just had to.

Chapter Eighteen

April worked hard to concentrate on the little girl sitting on the exam table at the clinic, her mouth opened wide. April pointed her exam light into the back of her throat seeing exactly what she'd expect. Swollen, red tonsils and a red throat. She pressed the sides of eight-year-old Amy's throat. "Is that sore?"

Amy winced. "Yes. It hurts to swallow."

She put down the light and smiled. "I imagine it does. Good job sitting so still and taking directions. You're an excellent patient."

The little girl beamed. "I'm going to be a nurse when I grow up."

"That's wonderful. We need a lot of good nurses, and I'll bet you'll be very good at it." April turned to the girl's mother. "Her lungs and heart are excellent, but her tonsils are inflamed and swollen. We need to get them out."

Amy frowned. "What do you mean? Is that bad?"

"No. you'll be fine. Come on. I'll help you

down, and we can talk on the way out." She took Amy's hand to steady her as she jumped off the exam table and then held open the door for the pair and followed them out. "I'll have the front desk schedule the surgery and get in touch with you." Pausing, she leaned over to meet Amy's eyes. "You'll get to eat all the ice cream and Jell-O you want after those tonsils are gone. I'll bet your mom will get your favorite flavors for you if you ask nicely."

Amy bounced on her toes and clapped her hands. "Yay! Can I, Mom?"

Her mother smiled and stroked Amy's long blond hair. "Absolutely. We'll buy at least three of your favorites."

"Then I want to have them out today, okay?" Amy looked up at April.

She laughed. "Sorry, kiddo, not today, but soon." April glanced up at the sound of a throat clearing a few feet away.

Dr. Schneider stood there tapping his toes, his arms crossed over his narrow chest and his brows raised. He took a folder out from under his arm and stepped closer, totally ignoring her patient.

The mother looked from him to April. "Thank you, Dr. Monroe. We'll be on our way."

April glanced at the file the doctor shoved into her hand. "What's this?"

"A new patient. Please don't keep her waiting any longer. You're already five minutes past her appointment time. She's in room 207."

"I'll be right there." She flipped open the file as the doctor huffed and strode down the hallway. As her gaze landed on the name of the patient, her shoulders stiffened, and she sucked in a quick breath. Could she possibly hand this one off to another doctor? She looked up and down the hall and then decided. No. Better to get this over so she could move on with her life once and for all.

April pushed open the door at room 207 and stopped, still not quite willing to believe what she saw.

Esther Hardin rose from the chair where she'd been sitting, her hands gripped tightly in front of her. "Hello, April."

"Mrs. Hardin." She nodded and strode to the small laptop on the far side of the room, sitting on the stool and flipping it open. "Thank you for coming. I don't have your medical records here, but I have a feeling there might not be much on file for you in your hometown, regardless." She waved at the chair. "Please have a seat."'

The older woman remained standing. "April, I'd like to have a word with you."

April blanched. The last thing she wanted was another discussion of any kind with Jesse's mother. She'd had more than enough of that back at the farm. "Let's start with a routine checkup." She pushed to her feet. "If you don't mind sitting on the exam table, I need to listen to your heart and lungs." She flipped open the file again and reviewed it. "It looks like the nurse took your blood pressure and pulse, and those look normal."

"April." Mrs. Hardin held out a hand. "Please."

"I'm not sure what we have to discuss, Mrs. Hardin. Can you tell me what symptoms you've been having that brought you in today?" She gestured toward the exam table again. "Please have a seat here."

Mrs. Hardin sighed but stepped up onto the low bench below the table and sank onto the cushioned area of the exam bed. She waited patiently while April listened to her heart and checked her ears and throat.

"Take a deep breath please." April placed

the stethoscope on Mrs. Hardin's back. "Now let it out." She moved it to another place. "Thank you. Again please."

"Naomi got her stitches out yesterday, April. She asked that I send her deepest apologies for what she said to you about Jesse."

April pressed her lips together to keep the words from spilling out that she knew she shouldn't say.

"She asked that I tell you that what she said to you were all lies fostered from a spirit of jealousy. She feels very badly and doesn't wish that you and Jesse would quarrel."

April walked over to the laptop, slid onto the stool to record her findings, then looked up. "There is no me and Jesse, Mrs. Hardin. Naomi may have spoken from a place of jealousy, but she was still correct. Jesse's place is with his family. I'm not the right woman for him. I would only bring division into his life, not peace or happiness. I left because it was the right thing to do. Naomi might not be the best woman for him, but I'm not either." She dropped her hands into her lap and met the older woman's gaze. Then she returned her attention to the laptop, hoping Mrs. Hardin would finish her apology on Naomi's behalf and leave. It was obvious she didn't need anything for herself, since she didn't seem open to discussing any medical needs.

"Naomi is not the only person who needs to apologize to you, April. I do too."

April's attention jerked up from the laptop screen, and she stared at Mrs. Hardin. "What did you say?"

"I said I owe you an apology, and probably much more so than Naomi ever did. I never gave you a chance when you came to our home with Jesse." She slipped off the table and walked to one of the two chairs against the wall and sank into it. "I always hoped Jesse would return home, especially after his daed passed. Amish are very hard-headed, often stubborn people, who believe they know what is best. As I'm sure you have observed, change is difficult for us." She gripped her hands in her lap and knotted them together. "But I have seen your kindness, your generous spirit, your compassion for other people even if they are strangers. Most of all, I have seen your love for my son, and I am deeply sorry for how I treated you, April. I pray you can find it in your heart to forgive me."

"Mrs. Hardin, I . . ." April was at a loss for what to say.

"Please. Call me Esther?"

"Thank you . . . Esther." She stood and took a step closer to the older woman. "I do forgive you, with all my heart. I understand how a mother would feel the way you do, and I accept your apology. I know it's not customary for Amish people to hug an Englischer, but would you mind if I give you a hug?" Her heart beat fast in her chest, and she partly extended her hands, wondering if she'd be rejected yet again.

Esther took a small step toward her, seeming to hesitate for a second. Then she smiled. "I think I would like that, ya."

A few seconds later, April pulled back and stepped away. "Wait. How did you get here? You surely didn't drive your buggy all the way from home."

A slow smile lit Esther's face. "Nein. I did not. I had a driver who is to meet me at Central Park. Is it far from here? I would love to see it. From what I have heard, it's the only place in this huge city that has any green grass or trees. It will help me feel more at home. Are you off soon and might you walk me there?"

April glanced at her watch. "You're actually my last patient for the day, but I'd like to suggest something before we leave, if you're willing."

Esther tipped her head to the side. "Ya? What is it, April?"

"I know you don't like doctors, but since you're here, would you consider taking a quick blood test to check for diabetes? I can have the results sent to Jesse if you'd like, after I take a look at them. And if it is diabetes, maybe you'd consider being treated at the same hospital where Naomi went?"

Esther seemed to consider for several long moments then she gave a very slow nod. "After what you did to help Naomi, I trust you, April. Ya. I will do that if we can do it quickly."

April smiled. "We have a lab right down the hall and I can walk you there and wait while blood is drawn. Just a moment and I'll type up the order so the lab has it and knows where to send the results." She swung back around to her laptop and entered the necessary instructions then stood. She considered for a moment, not sure how she felt about walking with Esther Hardin to Central Park. It was only a ten-minute brisk walk, but she was feeling a bit tired after the emotional roller-coaster she'd experienced the last few minutes. Maybe it would be kinder to take that walk and then put all of this behind her. "All right. I'd be happy to walk with you to meet your driver after we finish at the lab." That might be stretching her sentiments a bit, but it was the right thing to do. After all, Esther had come all this way to apologize, and the least she could do was give her a few more minutes of her time.

Thirty minutes later, they hit the edge of the park. Esther stopped and looked around. "Look at all the horses and buggies! I had no idea the Englisch used these for transportation."

April bit back a smile. "It's actually more for people who have never ridden in a horse-drawn buggy and want to experience it for the first time."

"They pay money to ride in a buggy? How interesting." Esther stopped near a horse and reached up to stroke its nose. "You are a pretty one." She nodded at the driver. "You have a handsome gelding, sir."

He tipped his hat. "Thank you, ma'am. He's been a good horse for me these past few years."

"Do you treat him well? Give him clean hay and good quality grain? Plenty of water and rest when he needs it? Keep up on his hoof care and brush him often?"

"Yes, ma'am." He straightened his shoulders

and maintained a serious expression. "That I do. He provides both our livelihoods, and he's treated like royalty at my house."

"That is goot." Esther waved a hand and stepped onto the grass over the nearby curb. "Come along, April. My driver will be waiting."

April hurried to catch up, still marveling over the exchange she'd heard between Esther and the driver. No doubt the driver hadn't encountered very many Amish who took the time to stop and question his treatment of his horse. "Are you going home tonight, Mrs. . . . Esther?" It still felt strange to use her first name. A jogger moved at a fast pace down a path beside them, going the opposite direction. That reminded April—she still needed to keep her word and go for a jog with May. Somehow, the thought didn't bring the joy it had before leaving for Jesse's home.

"I do not think so. I believe I'm staying in town for the night and then possibly going home tomorrow, but I'll know more a little later." She moved along with a brisk stride that April had to work to keep up with. This little woman had more energy than she did, at least this afternoon.

"Ah, there he is." Esther slowed her pace

and pointed ahead toward a set of steps leading up to a terrace full of greenery and flowers.

A man rose from the steps and took a step into the light. April's heart lurched and then felt as though it had stopped for a couple of seconds. "Jesse."

Jesse stood under a tree that had lost over half its leaves, and the remaining few were muted oranges and reds. He gazed at April, hoping she could see his love reflected in his eyes and wondered if she'd turn and leave or give him a chance to explain.

She took a tentative step, glanced at his mother, and then back at him. "Jesse? I didn't expect to see you here. You're back in New York? I somehow thought you'd stay at the farm a bit longer."

He merely nodded, then he closed the distance between them and opened his arms, praying with all his might that she'd respond the way he hoped. "There was something much more important here."

April's mouth curved into a small smile. She flew across the intervening distance and launched herself into his embrace, soft sobs coming from the region of his heart as she buried her face in his chest.

He stroked her hair. "Shh. It's all right. I'm so sorry you were hurt and left the farm. I should have done more to protect you, to make it a happy time for you, not something to fear or run from."

April eased back a little but didn't release her hold on him. "I thought I was doing the right thing for you. I didn't want to come between you and your family. Then Naomi said . . ." She placed her hand over her own lips and shook her head. "It doesn't matter. Your mother told me Naomi apologized and said she was wrong. That means a lot." She peeked over at Jesse's mother, standing a discreet distance away. "Then Esther came to the clinic and made an appointment to see me. I suppose you knew she was going to do that?"

He nodded. "I dropped her at the front door and told her if all went well, to please ask you to take a walk to show her Central Park and to meet her driver. I assume you received what she came to say?" He bent down and placed a tender kiss on her forehead then straightened, meeting her gaze.

"Yes. She said she was sorry and hadn't meant to drive me away. That she saw my love for her son . . ." Soft rose color flooded her cheeks, and she dipped her head.

Jesse placed his finger under her chin and lifted her face to meet his. "So you do love me still? Even after everything that happened?"

"Yes. Very much. That's why I left, because your happiness is more important to me than my own."

This time he placed a soft kiss on her cheek. "I had to try again, April. I couldn't give up on you . . . on us. When Maam told me she wanted to come in person to apologize, I jumped at the chance to drive her and come see you again since you weren't answering my calls."

She seemed to stiffen in his embrace, but only for a moment. "I'm sorry, but I didn't see the point. I felt it was best to end things, not drag them out."

"I totally get that. I never should have kept my past a secret for so long. That's where things got off track for us. If I'd been honest up front, let you have time to absorb the idea before springing it on you right before I took you home, it might have been easier. I have to admit I was scared. We come from two different worlds, and I wasn't sure how you'd take the news that I'd been raised Amish. I started falling for you the first time we met at the coffee shop, and when you came into my clinic with that hurt puppy, I was a goner. There never seemed to be a good time to broach the subject." He brushed a tendril of hair off her cheek and tucked it behind her ear. "I believe we can make it work, April. We have to, because I don't think I can live without you."

A smile broke across her face. "I agree. I feel the same way."

Jesse glanced over at his maam and saw her nod and smile while she seemed to be brushing away a stray tear. The sight warmed his heart, and he didn't hesitate another moment. He dropped to one knee while he fished in his pocket for the small box he'd kept there the last few days. "April." He took a deep breath and tried again. "Dr. Monroe." He held out the box and opened the lid. "I love you with all my heart and soul. If you'll have me, I promise to cherish you, protect you from harm, and be faithful to you for the rest of my life. Will you marry me?" He could almost hear his heart pounding in his chest as he waited for her reply.

April gasped. "Yes! Oh, yes, yes, yes! Of course, I'll marry you." She giggled and extended her hand. "Dr. Hardin." She waited for him to slip the ring onto her finger. With her other hand, she pulled him to his feet and flung her arms around him.

This time he aimed for her lips and gave her a long, slow, heartfelt kiss that he hoped would speak everything he was struggling to say.

After a few more seconds, April looked at his mother. "Do you agree, Esther? Do we have your blessing?"

Esther walked over slowly, and her face broke into the most beautiful smile Jesse had seen in years. "Ya. My deepest blessing. I am very happy for you both. Welcome to our family, April." She opened her arms and drew both of them into a hug.

April gave a soft sigh a minute later. "There's just one condition, Dr. Hardin."

"Name it. Whatever it is, I agree." Jesse would give this woman the moon if she asked for it.

"We're moving back home where you belong. Not to the farm, but to Bird-in-Hand."

Jesse heard his mother gasp and start to cry, and suddenly, he knew that all was right in his world, no matter what might come in the future.

Epilogue

Nine Months Later . . .

DRS. JESSE AND APRIL HARDIN STOOD holding hands in the small town of Bird-in-Hand, gazing with pride at the glass-fronted brick building with two glass doors one on the right and one on the left of the front wall. On one door was etched, Jesse Hardin, DVM, Veterinarian Clinic and on the other, April Hardin, M.D., Private Practice, General Practitioner. April tightened her grip on Jesse's hand as she tried to take in the dream that was coming to fruition before them. Who would have believed two years ago that she'd meet this amazing man and move to Amish country?

Rachel, Esther, Levi, Sarah, May, and Rob stood flanking them on both sides. Rachel let out a little squeal and clapped her hands. "I'm so excited for you . . . and for us." She looked at her mother who nodded. "For all of us that you're going to live here where we can see you so often. Plus, it was so fun getting to attend an Englischer wedding. It was beautiful, and I loved the music. But I think when I get married, I plan to stay with our traditional Amish wedding. It's so simple, and well, just right."

"Ya, I agree. It was a lovely wedding." Esther placed a gentle hand on April's shoulder. "April, my new daughter, I am so proud to have you in our family."

"Thank you, Esther. That means so much." April squeezed the older woman's hand and then grinned at Rachel. "Do you have someone in mind for that future wedding, Rachel?"

Rachel ducked her head, but April could see color flood the girl's face. "If I did, I wouldn't tell. We keep those things a secret, you know."

May waited a moment and then walked around and faced April. "We have news too. Actually, double news." She glanced at Rob who gave her two thumbs up. "We've decided we don't want to raise our son and our new baby in the city, and we're going to see what we can do about moving here too. I can't stand the thought of being so far from my sister and her new husband."

April's eyes widened. "New baby? Moving?

What?" She tried to take it all in. She emitted a squeal that would rival Rachel's and pulled May into a big hug. "Oops. I'd better not hug you too tight, huh, I remember you had morning sickness with Zack. When is the baby due? Are you having any morning sickness this time? Does Zack know yet? Rob can work at home, but what about you?" All the questions came out so fast that everyone in their small group started to laugh.

May pulled back and patted her flat stomach. "Not for another seven months. We just found out, and so far, so good on how I'm feeling. Zack knows and is already trying to think of names for his little brother. He's determined it will not be a girl." She grinned. "Rob can work at home, and I'm not going to work at all. I plan to be a full-time mom from now on. It's going to be so much less expensive living here than in New York, that we'll be fine on one salary."

Rob placed an arm around May's shoulder and drew her close. "I've wanted her to quit since Zack was born, and now it feels like the right time. She'll give notice after we find a house here and know when we're going to move."

Jesse reached out a hand to Rob and shook his. "That's wonderful, or wunderbar, as the Amish say. It's going to be so nice for April to have part of her own family here."

April felt as though her cup of joy couldn't get any fuller, and she sent up a prayer of thanksgiving. God had been so good to her this past year, and she decided right then that she was going to make it her life's work to serve Him while she also served the people in this community.

Levi clapped Rob on the back. "I agree. Having family close is a wonderful thing. We welcome you to the community, and I look forward to getting to know you both better."

Sarah smiled and nodded. "Me too." She reached out and hugged April. "It will be nice to have a doctor that we trust in the area when my little one comes along." She placed her hand on her belly and gazed with adoration up at her husband.

Rachel was bouncing on her toes. "I'm so glad you finally told them. I was about to burst with the news. Two new babies in the community, and both of them coming close to the same time. April is going to be busy with her new patients."

April laughed and slipped her hand into Jesse's again. "Speaking of which, how about we go inside and see our new digs?"

"You don't have to ask me twice. Let's go. Come on, everyone. You can help us celebrate inside. There's cake, coffee, and rhubarb pie in April's office."

"Yes, and I baked that pie all by myself." April peeked over at her mother-in-law, wondering what she'd say.

Esther drew herself up and lifted her chin. "I am guessing it will be the best pie we have ever eaten, for sure and for certain. But I shall need to be careful, since the doctor said I can't eat much in the way of sweets, after discovering I do have diabetes. Maybe one small piece to celebrate your new lives, ya?"

April slipped her hand through the older woman's arm and squeezed. "This doctor thinks that would be fine." She surveyed her mother-in-law with love and pride warming her heart. "I can't believe how wonderful you look. You're slim and so much stronger now, and you walk with more confidence. I'm so glad you decided to get that blood work done when you came to New York."

"Ya. I am too." Esther beamed at her, pride clearly showing in her eyes. "I am glad for many things, but my biggest joy is having my family back together, and my new daughter by my side."

Printed in the USA
CPSIA information can be obtained
at www.ICGtesting.com
LVHW010746310324
775971LV00039B/1442